April 23, 2016

TANGLEVILLE

Just About Any Town, Anywhere

DONALD H. HULL

To Marlene Vollons,
— God's servant.
Don H+

◆ FriesenPress

Suite 300 - 990 Fort St
Victoria, BC, Canada, V8V 3K2
www.friesenpress.com

ISBN
978-1-4602-7705-8 (Hardcover)
978-1-4602-7706-5 (Paperback)
978-1-4602-7707-2 (eBook)

1. Fiction, Christian

Distributed to the trade by The Ingram Book Company

I don't know if Donald Hull has read Carl Jung's *Man in Search of a Soul*, but in *Tangleville* he puts flesh on Jung's observation that most people who have reached their forties without having acquired any substantive conclusions about their life goals or a viable working faith become increasingly neurotic. Lacking a clear vision about themselves or of their ultimate future, they find flying by the seat of their pants increasingly difficult and unsatisfying, striking out in various ways to hide or compensate for what is ultimately their frustrated spiritual development. In *Tangleville* Hull plays off the apparently successful, the drunk, the battered partner, and the emotionally and intellectually insecure against their opposites. It's a fascinating read and so is the psychology that underlines real and substantive understanding that, interestingly, makes life worth living and living well. It's a tale that can be set any time, any place, anywhere.

The Rev. Frederick Eldridge, MA, Deacon and Spiritual Director

A redemption tale, yes, but with a fresh process, as we tread alongside Canon Steadmore on his pastoral journey. Christians and non-Christians alike will enjoy the insights into how a committed rector deals not only with the concerns and conflicts of the parishioners and non-parishioners of his parish, but also into the inner dialogue of Canon Steadmore as he and his wife evaluate and re-evaluate his motivations and goals. As enjoyable a sermon as you will ever receive in novel form!

Graham Parker, Ph.D., Professor, Division of Pediatric Neurology, Dept. of Pediatrics, Wayne State University

Harry Sting, a dynamic radio show host, treads on thin ground as he begins a series of interviews with the refreshingly honest and forthright Canon Steadmore. It isn't long before Harry Sting discovers that the ratings of his radio show aren't the only thing he needs to be worried about. Harry takes a chance and confides in Canon Steadmore, only to find that his life is changing in ways he could not have imagined.

The residents of Tangleville show us that people can change when they realize that there is a better way to live their lives.

Joyce Zuk, MA, Executive Director,
Family Services Windsor-Essex

Looking for a story of a modern clergyperson's ministry within contemporary Canadian Society? You will be given insight into a senior parish priest's daily routine, highlighting his connection to his parish members and his family life. It is the story of the Reverend Canon Doctor Barclay Steadmore, most of all through the drama with Harry Sting and his daily radio talk program where the issues between secular society and the faith and belief of the Christian are explored. The critique of relative issues of all society and those of atheism and agnosticism will be found to be clear and carefully expressed.

Read, enjoy, be uplifted and challenged!

The Right Reverend Jack Percy Peck, MA, DD,
retired bishop of the Anglican Diocese of Huron

"The law indeed was given through Moses;
grace and truth came through Jesus Christ."
John 1:17 NRSV

This book is dedicated to all Christians in this secular age who struggle living out their faith in Jesus Christ. Grace and truth through Christ must prevail in all matters, for our Lord said:

"For this I was born, and for this I have come into
the world, to testify to the truth. Everyone
who belongs to the truth listens to my voice."
John 18:37 NRSV

FOREWORD

THE author of *Tangleville* has added grace and structure to my ministry and life for over twenty-five years. It all came about by a chance meeting one day in a hospital corridor when the then Reverend Donald H. Hull said to me, "I think I need to change my direction." I replied, "Well, let's have a coffee and talk about it." The eventual result of that conversation was that he became my successor in the great ministry of the Church of the Ascension in Windsor, Ontario.

As I have read and re-read this book I see him changing the direction of others as he encounters them in his ministry. Canon Donald Hull has built his life on pointing people in a new direction.

The farm boy, who became a high school math teacher, a United Church minister, an Anglican priest, college principal, and university lecturer, is now an author. This book has by word, ministry, and example, followed the admonition of Jesus: "I am the way, the truth, and the life," and, "Follow me."

Canon Hull takes the ministry of St. Bartholomew's Church out of the church building into the town radio station, then into the heart and mind of the controversial Harry Sting, bringing him comfortably back to the front pew of St. Bart's. The characters in this book are fictitious, but they are, in fact, all alive and well in every church and community.

God hears the prayer of Annie, Harry's devoted wife, and plants His purpose into the heart and mind of Canon Doctor Barclay Steadmore, who takes the plan and, with His strength, not only converts Harry Sting, but places him at the heart of a badly needed sacred mission in the heart of Tangleville.

"Remember who you are," Barclay's wife tells him as he nervously readies himself for the first interview. He reminds himself that he is child of God, a member of Christ, and an inheritor of the Kingdom of Heaven.

Do you see a St. Bartholomew's in your town? Do you see your radio station with its own version of Harry Sting being able to reverse the trend? Are you a Harry Sting waiting to change your lifestyle? Is there a Red Pagoda as a meeting place where you can make a commitment?

The plan that unfolds in this book is not a fictitious notion in the mind of Canon Doctor Donald Hull…it reflects what his mission is: tackling head on the way people think and equipping them for Life in Christ. God is working his purpose out and through this book others will come to know God and make Him known.

The Venerable Doctor Ronald Matthewman,
Archdeacon of Essex Deanery, Anglican Diocese of Huron (retired)

Acknowledgments

THIS novel is the coming together of many years of having the great privilege of being an Anglican priest, preparing weekly sermons, celebrating the sacraments, thought-provoking discussions with wise and close friends, receiving the love of wonderful parish congregations, and decades of questions fermenting in the background of my Christian journey to date.

For some time there was the search for a vehicle to be used to bring to the surface some method of conveying to others, those who perhaps struggle with their own understanding of the Gospel of Christ, a format to argue the relevance of Christian theology in a modern secular society. The result was the creation of a fictional small town named Tangleville, a place where ordinary people exist, wrestle with their faith...or lack of faith, and try to cope with the ups and downs of being human.

There are many to whom I owe deep thanks and appreciation for making this book possible: my upbringing by my loving, Christian parents (now deceased) and to the Rev. Gervais Black and the Venerable Dr. Ronald Matthewman, two long-time mentors and clergy role models. Special thanks to my family for the encouragement they gave to write this undertaking.

To Gillian Stefanczyk, one of the very few people who can read my handwriting and whose keyboard skills and patience in typing the manuscript made the entire work possible, a million thanks!

I express deep appreciation to Thom Smith, my editor. To the four individuals who took the time to read and write reviews of the original work: Rev. Frederick Eldridge, Dr. Graham Parker, Ms. Joyce Zuk, and the Rt. Rev. Jack Peck. And, of course, to the Venerable Dr. Ronald Matthewman who penned the Foreword, providing background content to the reader.

John Stuart Mill, 1806-1873, wrote the following:

> *"There must be discussion, to show how experience is to be*
> *interpreted. Wrong opinions and practices gradually yield*
> *to fact and argument: but facts and arguments, to produce*
> *any effect on the mind, must be brought before it."*

In our modern secular society, there is no greater need for clarity in opinions and convictions than in the realm of one's relationship with God. It is my hope that this novel may, in the words of John Stuart Mill, instill an "effect on the mind" to produce mature and faithful servants of Jesus Christ.

CHAPTER ONE

BARCLAY Steadmore was anxious…he could see it in his reflection as he stood before the bathroom mirror, face lathered for his morning shave. Why had he ever accepted that invitation way back in the fall? "It's easy," he thought to himself, "to say 'yes' when the consequences of a quick reply are so many weeks into the future." But now the day of reckoning had come.

"This is ridiculous," he reminded himself. After all, he had stood behind the pulpit, Sunday after Sunday, for the last twenty years. He had spoken before large crowds at many weddings, funeral services, public meetings, and civic events more times than he could remember, bringing greetings and off-the-cuff speeches on demand. The fact that he'd already cut himself twice so far in his daily ritual of scraping off his visible stubble proved the existence of his anxiety.

"Hurry dear, or you'll be late." The words of his wife Faith echoed up the stairway and through the partially closed bathroom door. He knew she was right. Normally, Barclay Steadmore was early for every appointment and event in his life. But not today.

Since it was to be a thirty-minute radio interview at the local station downtown, Barclay didn't bother to put on his clerical collar that morning. After all, aside from the host and the radio station crew, who would see him? It wasn't, he reminded himself, a television performance. Besides, Barclay wanted to be as comfortable as possible that morning. Sometimes the clerical collar seemed so restrictive.

Faith Steadmore was already at the front door of their modest but comfortable home. "Good luck, dear. Watch out for that Harry Sting. Just remember who you are and you'll do fine. I'll be listening at ten o'clock."

"Just remember who you are." Faith's words continued to race through his mind as he drove the quick ten-minutes to radio station AM KNOW. Maybe that was his problem, he thought to himself. Did he really…really…know who he was? If he did, then why was he so worried?

As Barclay wound through the light traffic of Tangleville his mind was anywhere but on his driving. His thoughts drifted back over the already too quickly passed fifty-one years of his life to his early days on the farm as a young boy, growing up the oldest of three children in the family Steadmore.

The memories were as clear as if they had happened only last week. He hadn't thought about it for years, but one incident from his youth seemed to flash into his mind and preoccupy his thoughts. He was fourteen years old again and it was smack in the middle of January. He was walking down the quarter-mile lane of the family farm, knee deep in freshly fallen snow, trudging to the highway to catch the school bus to take him the twenty-mile one-way trip to the county high school. He had a tuque pulled way down over his ears to protect his neck and his closely cropped haircut. Brush cuts were in vogue in those days. Every self-respecting boy had one and Barclay was no different. But it was that tuque that was the big problem of the day. His mother had made him wear it, and it was absolutely a social "no-no" for him. "You'll catch your death of pneumonia, Bark," she'd say every day of the week. "So wear it!"

"Bark" was what everyone called him at home. He hated that too! But there wasn't much he could do about it. So as long as he was within sight of the family home, that tuque stayed on his head. Besides, at twenty degrees below Fahrenheit, it was a welcome piece of material to protect him from the biting January wind.

Barclay could remember it as clearly as he could make out the license plate of the Land Rover in front of him. Just as soon as that big old yellow Ford school bus would appear over the hill, off that red and blue and white tuque would come to be stuffed into his school bag, not to appear until his exit from the bus about 4:30 each evening, permitted to protect him from the wind and snow as he trudged back up the lane to the Steadmore farm house. "Mother would never know the difference." he always thought to himself. "Keep her happy…that's all that matters. Hats are made to go on, and they're made to come off."

The Land Rover ahead of him had jammed on its brakes and Barclay Steadmore was back to reality. He flipped on the car radio and, wouldn't you know it, he heard his own name broadcasted over the airwaves. He hadn't heard the spot before, but others in the parish had told him they had:

> "We continue our 10:00 a.m. series today, trying to wrestle with the complicated issues of faith and morality in our fast-changing world. Each week a local religious leader is invited to come and discuss matters of religion and faith with Harry Sting. This week, The Reverend Canon Doctor Barclay Steadmore, Rector of St. Bartholomew's Anglican Church in downtown Tangleville, is our featured guest.

Don't miss it! We invite you, the listening audience, to call in after the show to express your opinions of what has been said."

"Ouch," thought Barclay. "This could be a disaster." He had never met Harry Sting. But Harry's tough interviewing reputation and his reported disdain for things religious had guaranteed that his listening audience was growing at a faster rate than any other station in the area. "Am I just more fodder for the day?" Barclay thought to himself. He didn't want to be used, and certainly he didn't want the good name of St. Bart's and other Christians' faith in God to become merely entertainment for the disbelieving listeners.

Barclay anxiously checked his watch. It was nine twenty-five. As he pulled into the parking lot, there was exactly one open parking space remaining. A Chevrolet Corvette was just leaving ahead of him. "Perhaps this is a good sign," he thought to himself. "Maybe this won't be so bad after all." He knew that he wouldn't say that out loud to anyone, but maybe God was looking out for him in spite of his personal lack of self-confidence. He glanced ahead at the front doors of radio station: AM KNOW, Voice of the Heartland.

Does God do that kind of thing? Is God that concerned about individuals that even parking spaces are provided for his followers? Now he was into theological matters. What if Harry Sting was to ask that kind of question on the show in a few minutes from now? Barclay put it out of his mind. The receptionist inside the entrance of the building was smiling at him.

"Yes? May I help you?" She asked in that friendly, but paid professional voice that is all too common in our modern age. "I wonder, does she really want to help me?" Barclay thought to himself. "Just doing her job, of course."

"Good morning. I'm Barclay Steadmore and I'm supposed to be Harry Sting's guest on the ten o'clock show."

"Mr. Steadmore, please take a seat over there, and somebody will be with you in a second."

It had been a long time since someone had called him "Mr. Steadmore." Of course…he wasn't wearing his clerical collar. How would she know that he was a priest? Most folks he knew called him by one of his professional titles: Reverend, Father, Canon, Doctor, or some combination of the lot. But today, Barclay Steadmore was on secular ground, and he knew it.

While he waited in the lobby a sermon was already forming in his mind as the minutes ticked by. If a Christian doesn't wear some kind of a religious symbol, a cross, for instance, or a clerical collar, or some kind of a slogan on one's t-shirt or lapel, how are others to know that one is a Christian? Christians pretty well look like everyone else, at least on the exterior.

The formation of the whole sermon would have to wait for another time, because a rather efficient-looking young woman quickly approached him. "Hi, Mr. Steadmore. Thank you for coming today. I am Jennifer, the production co-ordinator. Please come with me. We only have ten minutes to airtime. Do you wish to use the bathroom before we go into the studio?" "No, thank you," Barclay replied. "It's only going to be a thirty-minute show, isn't it?"

There it was again…Mr. Steadmore. Of course, she was only being polite and politically correct. He meant nothing to her. She was just doing her job, getting him ready, setting him up before the microphone across the desk of the famous Harry Sting. She obviously had done this type of thing countless times before. Here was just another middle-aged sacrificial lamb to help Harry Sting fill the airwaves with chatter for the next half hour. Then he'd be gone and she'd be repeating it all over again with another guest for Harry tomorrow. Just another guest to come and go to help fill the insatiable appetites of the listening audience out there in radio land.

So did it really matter what he'd say today? The question raced through Barclay's mind. Did it really? Will anyone remember what he said thirty minutes after the show was off the air? Is this what our world has come to? If he was to be bland and predictable, then Harry's ratings wouldn't be helped and he himself would be labelled as just another example of a dull, spineless clergyperson who wouldn't take a stand on controversial issues. If on the other hand, he was to be confrontational and aggressive, then Harry could get into the act and really attempt to score some leverage in the battle for radio name recognition. "No matter which way I choose to play it, Harry wins," Barclay thought to himself.

To make matters worse, Barclay didn't know the script for the day. What were the questions Harry would most likely ask? He knew Harry was known for his dislike of anything that smacks of religion, morality, and tradition, He was clearly a secular liberal in most areas of life.

The big clock on the wall indicated it was now nine fifty-five and Harry Sting was still not behind his microphone. "Thank goodness for small favours. I still have a few seconds to work on it," Barclay encouraged himself. His mind raced back to that trudge down the farm lane to the school bus and that tuque. The departing words of his wife Faith seemed to ring in his ears again. "Remember who you are!" He thought of his days in front of grade nine through senior classes teaching high school mathematics. Math was so clean, so predictable. So cut and dried. If only life could be based on such predictable authority as how to solve a quadratic equation or how to translate some conic in the xy plane.

The broadcast booth was a much smaller area than Barclay had anticipated. A drinking glass was there on the table before him with a pitcher of ice water ready to be poured if a guest needed it. A glass wall separated Harry and his guests from the technician in the adjacent room. Sound tiles were everywhere, placed strategically to reduce echo and outdoor sounds. The clock was visible above the control room. The glass divider separated the rest of the broadcast area.

The grand entrance of Harry Sting interrupted Barclay's musings. The talk show host just nodded at Barclay, pulled his earphones over his thick crop of stylishly combed black hair, and looked at the fellow on the other side of the glass wall…the control room only about three feet away.

The technician on the other side of the glass was holding up his hand, five fingers in the air…now four…now three…two…one.

The "ON AIR" sign on the wall over the glass panel flashed.

CHAPTER TWO

HARRY'S controlled, modulated voice was smooth, professional, and confident.

"Good Morning, thinking people of Tangleville. We're glad that you have tuned in today to be part of The Harry Sting Show. This Monday morning we're continuing to explore the role of faith and religion in our fast-changing world. Does the message of the church really matter in today's age? Is religious faith just a left over from the past...a voice crying in the wilderness?

Today we welcome to the hot seat the Reverend Canon Doctor Barclay Steadmore, rector of downtown's St. Bartholomew's Anglican Parish. Good morning, Reverend. What do you say to all of that?"

"Good morning, Mr. Sting," replied Barclay. "Thank you for inviting me to be your guest today. By the way, do you know where that expression you just used came from?"

Barclay could see Harry's eyes narrow and the muscles around his lips tighten ever so slightly. "Which expression?." Harry snapped.

"The words 'a voice crying in the wilderness.' Those are the words the Scriptures use to describe John the Baptist preparing the way of our Lord. Isn't it interesting how Biblical expressions have become so ingrained into everyday speech? Often we quote the Bible and we don't even realize it."

"This was not the way it was supposed to be going." Barclay thought to himself. He'd already antagonized Harry and they were only forty-five seconds into the show.

As Barclay waited for Harry's comeback, his mind was racing. Why was he really here this morning? Was he secretly hoping for notoriety if he could publicly put this left-leaning public agitator in his place? To score a few debating points over the airwaves? To prove that a Christian, along with all the other faithful followers of Christ out there in the listening audience, could feel vindicated? That at least one of them could better the secular giant?

Barclay secretly knew that if he were to win this debate today… now in his mind it had reached the concept of debate…that it certainly wouldn't hurt next week's attendance at St. Bart's. And which clergyperson doesn't wish for a larger Sunday gathering in the pews? Why, there would be a good chance that if some of the radio audience agreed with him they'd be there next Sunday just to see what this fellow Steadmore looked like. The David who slew Goliath! And there could even be a good chance that those who objected to his position would also show up, maybe even to heckle him in the service. What is it they say? "No publicity is bad publicity"

But at the back of his mind was a far more sobering question…a question that he just couldn't ignore. Could it all possibly be about ego…about the enhancement of the self? Or was he really supposed to be here today to represent Christ, his Lord? He could, after all, argue that in putting down Harry Sting he was doing it for the good of the Church and for all listening believers who may be feeling that they have been losing out to the advances of an ever-creeping secular infringement on their lives.

There it was again. The hat problem! Barclay knew that today one hat had to be worn and one had to come off. Barclay knew which one he'd have to wear.

If it hadn't occurred to Barclay before, it was becoming obvious now that Harry had invited him to be a guest on his show because of his theological reputation in Tangleville: a conservative theologian who was taking stands on moral issues that were contrary to those of Harry's. Harry was in show business, after all, and he was making a name for himself by mocking anything and everything promoted by traditional Christianity. "Who better in Tangleville than myself," thought Barclay, "to be the victim of Harry's venom?" Barclay had caught parts of Harry's show from the past and was well aware of the tactics Harry would use on his program.

The voice of Harry Sting brought him back to reality: "Why don't you let me ask the questions and you answer them?" Harry retorted. There was an icy edge to his voice.

"Fair enough!" responded Barclay. "But just for the sake of establishing some common ground rules today, do you want me to wear my sacred hat, or my secular hat, during this show? To be consistent in my answers I can't wear both at the same time!"

"Well." responded Harry, "you're not wearing your clerical collar today. So for the sake of simplicity, why don't you, as you put it, wear your secular hat today?"

Barclay realized right away that Harry Sting really didn't understand his question about hats. But then again, why should he? That, of course, is the reason why the secular world just doesn't get it when church folk object to the ever-changing moral and ethical standards of the age. To wear a secular hat, or a sacred hat, means one's moral foundation must stem from two entirely different foundations. Like two ships passing in a foggy night, each may hear the hollow sounds of the foghorn, but one can really never make out the details of the superstructure of the other. The foghorns simply serve as a warning to stay out of the way of each other.

"Reverend Steadmore, you and I both know that times are changing. Peoples' beliefs are changing. The church no longer has the influence on society it once had. We are living in a multi-cultural society. Who has the right to tell me how to live my life?"

"You're absolutely right!" agreed Barclay. "No one has the right to tell you how to live. I couldn't agree more! You have nothing but choice...unlimited choices...before you. In today's society, nothing is ultimately wrong if you are willing to wait out the popular consensus of the age."

Barclay could see that this was not the answer that Harry expected. But after all, Harry had agreed that Barclay was to wear his secular hat during the show. So Barclay had decided that was exactly what he'd do...tackle each of Harry's questions from a secular perspective.

"But Reverend, surely you must agree that the world today is not the one in which we grew up as children. You and I can remember a time as young boys when Sunday shopping was not possible. There were no public casinos, no nudity in movies, no Sunday sports, no legal abortions, no same-sex marriages. The church labelled all these activities 'sin.' Look how much freedom we have today. Look how progressive we've become."

"There's no doubt our society has changed," replied Barclay. "But, Harry, you and I agreed a few minutes ago on a basis for our discussion today. You agreed that I was to wear my secular hat, and if I'm to wear it, so must you. Now that means if we are talking in secular terms, you can't use the word 'sin' in your conversation with me. In the secular world, 'sin' has no meaning other than what society defines it to be. Do you see what I mean?"

"No, I don't," Harry responded. "Why can't I use the word 'sin' if I wish? The term exists!"

"Because, Harry, the term 'sin,' according to the dictionary, means 'transgression of divine or moral law.' But since we have agreed to wear our secular hats today, then the notion of the divine...divine moral law...can't really enter into our conversation. You see, without God, there is technically no such thing as divine transgression. What you really mean by the word 'sin' is that something is 'politically incorrect' conduct, actions that are unacceptable for the moment, or the decade, or the century...conduct out of sync with the mores of the times. But, if one is willing to wait it out, that which is politically incorrect at the present time may be just fine, even admirable and readily acceptable, sometime in the future. Haven't you heard people say, 'You are just not ready yet for dot, dot, dot?' You fill in the blank, Harry. You see, in the sacred domain, something that is unacceptable, forbidden by God, i.e., 'sin,' always has been, is, and always will be 'sin.' But not so in secular society. Do you see what I mean?"

"You're just splitting hairs, Pastor!"

"Harry, it all boils down to the understanding of authority...fixed authority or fluctuating, evolving authority. We agreed to have our discussion this morning as secularists. So then, we have to exclude the notion of fixed authority, external to humanity, and focus only on authority that bubbles up from within society. Got it?"

Barclay continued: "The basis for secular societies' standards, by necessity, are flexible, adapting to the whims of the times, constantly evolving. That which was admirable, indeed right, yesterday can be out of phase today. What is correct today may be deemed wrong tomorrow. Who knows? What we consider so 'in' this morning may be laughable in the future? If this tape could be re-played fifty years from now it may be deemed naive, even absurd. Isn't this fun to discuss?"

Barclay was really getting into this discussion. Things were going well. It suddenly dawned upon him that he really wasn't as nervous as he expected he would be. He waited for Harry to continue. Instead, he was cut off by Harry's announcement:

"Friends, we break now for a short commercial. Don't go away. I will be back with our guest in two minutes."

Harry leaned back in his padded leather chair and glared across the table at Barclay. The OFF AIR sign meant that it was safe for Harry to speak freely.

"Steadmore, what in the world are you trying to do this morning? Where are you going with that kind of talk we just put up with for the past few minutes? I brought you on this show as a clergyman, and you've turned into a philosopher...a sociologist!"

It's amazing how the human mind can process a multitude of thoughts in mere moments of time. Spoken words drastically slow us down. But when ideas do not have to be fashioned into verbal phrases, or typed on the page, the rational side of humanity can function at an amazing pace.

This was the first time that Barclay was seeing the real, authentic Harry Sting. Before the show, they had not even spoken. On the air,

Harry had come off as the consummate professional, totally in charge. But now Barclay was exposed to Harry portrayed in a very different light. Was it all just an act? A staged persona that Harry projected over the air waves? Could it be that he was just as susceptible to fear and anxiety and stress as all mere mortals can be? After all, being a radio host was a job that required a certain creative personality to project to a listening audience. Harry was competing for airtime just as every other radio station personality must do around Tangleville. Harry needed a hook on which to hang his show every time he went on the air. Was it possible that the crusty exterior he projected from show to show was, in reality, thinner than Barclay had imagined?

Suddenly Barclay realized that as a Christian he had a responsibility to put Harry at ease, and to assure him that he wasn't out to sabotage his reputation or his image before the public. On coming to the show, he originally wanted to show Harry up. But not now.

"Harry, I want you to know that I'm really enjoying being your guest today. You may not realize it, but I was scared to death coming in here this morning. I'm not sure where the second half of the show is going, but I'll promise you one thing. I want us to be friends, not enemies. So don't worry about a hidden agenda on my part. I won't intentionally embarrass you before your audience."

Harry's glare had somewhat softened. "Thank you." he said, and turned once again to his microphone.

"Welcome back to The Harry Sting Show. Our guest this morning is Reverend Steadmore, rector of St. Bartholomew's Anglican parish in down-town Tangleville. If you're just joining us, Reverend Steadmore and I have been discussing how society has changed over the past fifty years. Religious faith does not seem to be guiding the decisions we are making in our age. If our great grandparents were still alive to witness that which in their

day and age were societal prohibitions, they would be shocked at what is now tolerated and applauded in our progressive society. I know, Reverend Steadmore, that you would agree with the use of the word 'progressive' to describe what is happening, wouldn't you?"

"Well Harry, we certainly are progressing in time. Time never takes a vacation. But the word progressive also means 'improving.' That is the definition of 'progressive' that is debatable this morning. And only time will tell."

"Then what is accountable for the massive changes we've witnessed in society during the last fifty years, Reverend Steadmore? They couldn't have all come about unless people apparently wanted such changes."

"Harry, let's focus on one of the basic tenets of secularism. Secularism has no need, indeed, has no reason to be concerned about things 'holy.' As such, the term 'holy' has no affiliation with things temporal. Now when the 'holy' is eliminated from everyday life, then people are free to dismiss the concept of the 'sanctity of life.' And with the 'sanctity of life' dismissed, then we're free to substitute anything we choose in its place. And we've done that. We've discovered its replacement: 'quality of life.' So secularism has replaced the concept of the 'holy' with the 'pleasure principle.'"

"Hold it! So what, Reverend Steadmore? Surely you're not suggesting that pleasure is an unworthy end to what it means to be human, are you?"

"Of course not, Harry! But who are you, or anyone else, once we've eliminated the concept of the divine…the holy…to tell your neighbor or me how and where to seek, to find, and to take pleasure? If there is not the concept of a permanent validity, a sacred component to standards of conduct within our flexible secular understanding of acceptable morality…that which is considered proper, God-instructed behavior in life…then you have to be tolerant of my choices, and I of yours. Haven't you noticed that the number one virtue in our age is now the concept of tolerance? About the worst thing anyone can say about someone else is that he or she is intolerant."

"But Reverend Steadmore, our society doesn't tolerate everything that takes place in our midst. We don't tolerate pedophilia. We don't allow polygamy to flourish. We certainly object to lying, stealing, cheating, and slander."

"Sure we don't, Harry! Lying, stealing, cheating, and slander would disrupt the normal routines of business and commerce. It is still to our advantage to enforce such conduct in society. But here is the rub of the matter. Stealing, lying, cheating, and slander were once considered transgressions against the divine realm. Eliminate the concept of the divine, the holy, and such matters then merely become issues of practicality. They suit us. We need them. But if one can argue that one's conduct does not affect others, is consensual and brings to the self and to one's partners pleasure, who are you, and who is society, to deny anyone the pursuit of pleasure? It's not as if something is inherently wrong. It is just that society is not yet ready for it. Remember, anything is possible in a society where there is not a permanent basis of divine morality. When it comes right down to it, it can be argued that without God in the picture, anything and everything is ultimately permissible."

It was surprising how Barclay was now feeling at ease behind the microphone. It suddenly dawned upon him that he was now calling Mr. Sting by his first name, 'Harry.' And Harry, somehow, didn't seem quite as confrontational as he appeared at the beginning of the show. "Could it be possible that he and I are actually enjoying one another?" thought Barclay. "Could it be that there was a purpose after all in his being there? That God was using The Harry Sting Show as a vehicle for the propagation of the Gospel, the Good News of Jesus Christ?"

Barclay could see the technician on the other side of the glass partition signalling to Harry. Obviously, time was closing in for the second half of the show. But there were so many other things yet to be said. Time would be the dictator, as it always is.

"Reverend Steadmore, we only have about thirty seconds remaining in the show. Obviously there's a great deal more you and I could talk about on this subject. You tricked me earlier when you asked me which hat you wanted me to allow you to wear today. Tell you what! How about coming back next Monday, to wear your 'sacred hat,' as you put it? What do you say to that?" The listening audience, of course, would never know, but Harry winked an eye at Barclay and with an impish grin, waited for the response.

"You've got a deal, Harry!" replied Barclay as he reached across the desk to grasp the hand of the famous Mr. Sting.

The ON AIR sign went out and Barclay Steadmore realized that he had survived.

CHAPTER THREE

IT was only a short distance between the parking lot of the radio station and Barclay Steadmore's office at St. Bartholomew's parish in downtown Tangleville. It was a beautiful day. The sun was shining, traffic was light, and Barclay found it easy to guide his three-year-old Jeep Liberty through the mid-morning flow of vehicles. In his mind things that morning had gone rather well...he had emerged a survivor from his encounter with Harry Sting. At least, that's the way he was assessing the situation. The car radio, tuned to AM KNOW, was softly babbling in the background. It was the local meteorologist giving the weather forecast following the mid-morning news. The news and weather always followed between the first half and the second half of The Harry Sting Show.

Barclay's musing about the first half of the show was cut short by the distinct voice of Harry Sting. Barclay quickly reached for the volume knob of his radio.

"Welcome back to the second half of this morning's show. I'm Harry Sting, inviting you, the listening audience, to participate in the next thirty-minute portion of my program. As you who regularly listen to my show will know, I call this segment of my show "Your Turn." It is your turn to comment. What did you hear our guest, Reverend Barclay Steadmore,

rector of St. Bartholomew's downtown Anglican Church, say? Do you agree with him? Did he have anything relevant to pass on this morning? Or was that first thirty minutes of airtime just a waste of time in this modern age in which we exist? I want to hear from you. The lines are jammed, it appears, but keep trying. We'll try to take as many of your calls as we can in the next thirty minutes."

"Well, here it comes." thought Barclay as he guided his Jeep into the drive-thru of the downtown doughnut and coffee shop. "A medium coffee with double cream." he shouted into the speaker system, and then proceeded to the window to pick up his order.

The lady at the window was set for a visit. Her name was Sarah Davis; she was one of his parishioners and she was ready to talk. Barclay glanced in his rear-view mirror, hoping another vehicle was behind him, waiting to pick up an order and pushing him out of the way. But no such luck. It was such bad timing for him to have to lend a listening ear, with the voice of Harry Sting and a guest that he was dying to hear coming through the radio speakers and Sarah's obvious need to unload something that was bothering her. Barclay reached for the volume control knob and switched off the radio. But his heart, the truth be admitted, betrayed his actions.

Barclay's mind was in overdrive…there has always been a part of the Christian faith that argues with the ego, and no one knows this better than a clergyperson. What does one do when the self pleads, "Let me be me. I need time to myself. I really don't want to deal with someone else's problems right now." It would be so easy to say, "For goodness sakes, get a hold of yourself, lady, and work out your own salvation."

There it was…the word "salvation." The word had so many different meanings, most of them tied into a spiritual context. What was it our Lord said?

Blessed are the merciful, for they will receive mercy. (Matthew 5:7)

Here was a lady who was hurting, right now. The merciful, translated "Christian," thing to do was to listen. But Barclay knew deep down inside it was really an act of martyrdom on his part to do so. He was dying to the self as he gave in to Sarah's request. He really wanted to listen to The Harry Sting Show, to hear what the audience was going to say during the half-hour call-in portion.

Seminaries try to teach prospective clergy that they must divide their time into segments: time for self, time for family, time for the parish. But it only takes a few months into a pastorate to learn how this well-intentional advice doesn't work.

Guilt. Every Christian knows about guilt. The internal war that so often rages is between "Let me do my thing" and "Thy will be done, Lord." It is something that has bothered thinking Christians for centuries. Does one own oneself, or not? Can one ever say "no" to the needs of others? The words of St. Paul to the Christians in Galatia are tucked away in one's inner being:

> *I have been crucified with Christ; and it is no longer I who live, but it is Christ who lives in me. And the life I now live in the flesh I live by faith in the Son of God, who loved me and gave himself for me. (Galatians 2:19-20)*

Barclay's mind was racing. It was as if he was in his office preparing to draft a Sunday sermon. On the mature Christian. So the mature Christian "dies to the self to bring life to others." Every seasoned Christian has had to wrestle with what it means to put the self into the basement and to give others the guest room. Guilt, mixed with love for Christ, often produces strange emotions: a little resentment, sometimes annoyance, sometimes even anger. It is true…the mature Christian sometimes envies one's fellow brothers and sisters in the faith who have recently discovered the joy of conversion and who have not yet had to deal with the cost of discipleship. "Jesus and me," sooner or later, must develop into "Jesus, me, and others." It always seems that when one encounters "others," somewhere in the background lies the possibility of a hidden cross to carry. Crosses are heavy and they can cause us to stumble.

Sarah passed the medium coffee with cream through the window and leaned as far as she could into Barclay's Jeep. "You've got to talk to Bill." she said, looking back over her shoulder to make sure no one inside was listening. "He threatened to beat me again last night. I've been crying all night. Can you tell that my eyes are red from hours of no sleep?"

"Sarah, you look fine! But looking like everything is okay is not the answer. We've talked about this before. You cannot continue to allow this to happen. My talking to Bill is not the solution. You've got to make the decision to postpone your upcoming marriage. You deserve to be treated with respect and dignity. If this kind of abuse is happening now, even before you're married, it's only going to get worse after you've exchanged your vows. We can go to the police right now and get a restraining order on him! I'll go with you!"

"No, Canon! Just talk to Bill, won't you?" Sarah pleaded. "I know Bill didn't mean it. Will you talk to him? Please?"

Barclay agreed he'd speak to Bill, again, but only if Sarah would take the first step. "You'll have to confront Bill and have him call for an appointment. You have to own that the problem exists." Barclay was not going to let her off the hook that easily, for Sarah desperately needed to begin to personally stand up to Bill. At least by confronting Bill and demanding that he call the parish office was a small step in the right direction.

To his great relief Barclay could see that another vehicle was waiting close to his rear bumper, ready to pick up an order. "Sarah, I'll be waiting for Bill's call. It is up to you to begin to assert yourself." Barclay said, as he inched away from the drive-thru window. "See you in church on Sunday!"

It was the old, old story, all too familiar to every seasoned pastor. A woman is in love with love and blind to the faults of her man of affection. It seems almost unnecessary to say it, at least out loud. But clergy know from years of dealing with troubled relationships that often just a few months following one's wedding vows the disenchanted bride will admit to her pastor that she thought that following the marriage she could change the faults of her mate. She'd teach him how to dress a little more smartly; she'd get him to change his table manners so that in public his annoying traits with a fork and knife would not embarrass her in the company of friends; she'd be able to work on improving his grammar and slowly purge him of his profanity, which was so often offensive, especially to females and sophisticated movers and shakers in the community.

But how rarely this proves to be the case. If anything, it is usually just the opposite. When two people are dating, even while living together before marriage, each wears one's best mask and sports one's shiniest shoes, so to speak. After the vows are exchanged and the flowers of the great day are wilted the real selves begin to emerge. The discovery is made that wilted flowers cannot be revived. It has been said that "marriage begins when a man and a woman become as one; the trouble starts when they try to decide which one."

So often during marriage preparation classes couples gleefully explain at the outset that there really is not much that they don't know about each other. After all, they are already living together. Whenever clergy hear this confession, one's radar antennae go up. For clerical counselors know that already that the intended marriage is off to a rough start. Contrary to popular myth, living together before marriage actually reduces the chance of a successful marriage; some studies suggest by ten percent.

"But how could this be true?" the surprised couple ask. Surely a trial living arrangement should tell them if they were compatible as a couple. The fallacy in such an argument lies in a few simple facts. First, there must already be some doubt about a lifetime commitment, or there wouldn't be the need for a trial living arrangement. Living together before marriage still involves a false presentation of the real self because of the fear that if one's partner is confronted with one's "warts and all" so to speak, he or she may opt out of the arrangement. The escape clause is always waiting in the wings to be exercised.

There it was again…the old hat problem! Until one is married, does a partner wear the hat of the projection of the image that is really the self, or does one wear the hat, so to speak, that pleases one's partner? Often, the real hat is only worn following "tying the knot."

Barclay remembered his old seminary professor saying that living together before marriage is always blind to the future, for each partner only experiences the other in the present. Real commitment, taking seriously one's wedding vows, must acknowledge those words, "For better, for worse, for richer, for poorer, in sickness and in health, until death we do part." But who, during those glorious days of youth, when sexual desires and physical attractiveness are at the top of one's shopping list in choosing one's desirable partner, who is ready to project twenty, thirty, forty, or more years into the future and can truthfully comprehend how one will be able to cope willingly with a disabled spouse, a marriage of financial hardship, or the possibility that one partner will have outgrown the other intellectually, socially, or professionally?

Barclay recalled a conversation that he had had with a former bishop who talked about a new expression that seems to have slipped into modern usage: "a starter marriage." He explained how a "starter marriage" is like the purchase of a starter house...one that will suffice until one can move up to a better one. Barclay never forgot that expression "starter marriage" and how that corresponds to living together before marriage. A trial run if you will!

It seems pretty obvious that if a couple lives together before marriage then one's moral values can't be said to be firmly guided by the teachings of Holy Scriptures. Hence, the wedding vows said before God Almighty, to promise to stay together "for the rest of our lives," may already be lacking in sincerity and integrity. And sometimes, in marriage, when times are rocky for committed Christians, the only thread remaining to hold the marriage together is the fact that each partner promised before God that their marriage vows were indissoluble. Vows that cannot be broken. So, for many Christians, the only solution is to seek help and to work things out.

Barclay, and his wife Faith had promised to each other, years ago, that if the marriage was to end in divorce it would be the other partner who would seek that separation. And both were so committed to the teachings of Holy Scriptures, and so determined that it would be the other one who broke the vows, that if the time ever did come, neither would give in. They were stuck with each other and common sense dictated that the best thing to do in such a case was to make every possible effort to find solutions to ease the level of stress. But even with the best of intentions, and with rock-solid faith, marriages do fail. That is the reality of life.

Barclay Steadmore knew that he had been mentally sermonizing again as he pulled into the parking lot of St. Bart's. Why, Sarah and Bill could be representative names of hundreds of couples in

Tangleville…couples planning to get married, or those who are living together before marriage hoping to beat the odds, or perhaps long-time married couples simply living out their wedding vows merely by tolerating each other from day to day. Whatever happened to Christ's message of self-sacrifice and sacrificial love…love that St. Paul, in 1 Corinthians 13:4, spoke of when he penned these immortal words:

> *"Love is patient; love is kind; love is not envious or boast-ful or arrogant or rude. It does not insist on its own way; it is not irritable or resentful; it does not rejoice in wrong-doing, but rejoices in the truth. It bears all things, believes all things, hopes all things, endures all things. Love never ends." (ICorinthians 13:4-8)*

What was to happen to Sarah and Bill?

Barclay Steadmore, empty paper coffee cup in hand, walked into the reception area of St. Bart's. Hannah Fisher, the parish secretary, was hard at work, the radio playing softly in the background. Hannah looked up, smiled, and handed him a handful of four-by-six-inch pieces of paper. Barclay knew what they were: telephone calls to be made. Obviously, the office had been busy following The Harry Sting Show on AM KNOW.

"Tangleville has been aroused." teased Hannah. "Why don't you have a cup of tea before you face the rest of the day?"

"Let's do that." Barclay replied. "I think I'm going to need it!"

Chapter Four

WITH his cup of green tea, no sugar and no milk, placed on its usual spot…the upper right hand corner of the large monthly desk planner that outlined his appointments for the month…Barclay settled down to begin to work his way through the pile of telephone calls handed to him by Hannah.

There was one from Bill Stern, the peoples' warden, with the word "urgent" and his telephone number printed neatly at the bottom. "It must be serious." thought Barclay, "if Bill wants to be interrupted at the office."

There were calls from at least five of his parishioners. One was from a fellow priest over at St. Timothy's Parish across town. Another three included names he didn't recognize, and one was from the local newspaper *The People's Voice*. "That one will have to wait" Barclay thought to himself. "They smell a controversial story and they are looking for a sacrificial lamb to slaughter. Maybe I'll get around to it sometime by Friday," Barclay mused, a cynical smile crossing his lips.

There was no call from Bill Bilker, but perhaps it was still too soon, or too much to expect, that Sarah would have been able to convince him to make an appointment. "I will give them time," thought Barclay. "But I won't hold my breath."

One call needed to be made before any of the others, a call to Faith. She had promised to listen to The Harry Sting Show, and Barclay valued her opinions more than those of anyone else. Faith had a way of being brutally honest, something few people are able to do when speaking to clergy. After thirty years of marriage, there was no need for pretence or political correctness in their relationship. If Faith had an opinion as to how the show went, Barclay needed to hear it before he talked to anyone else.

His home phone rang, and it seemed like forever before Faith picked it up.

"So, what's the verdict?" Barclay asked.

"Well, let me put it this way!" Faith replied. "You certainly stirred up a hornet's nest in Tangleville. I've never heard so many people taking such radically opposite sides in their points of view. Harry's second half of the show was the most rambunctious I've ever heard in months. His ratings certainly won't suffer. I'm just worried about the fallout at St. Bart's. How are you doing?"

"Give me the bottom line, Faith. Just 'thumbs up' or 'thumbs down.' That's all I need before I get to this stack of calls to be made."

"Thumbs up, Rector! But just remember, now you've got a town full of Harry Stings to deal with. You certainly know who you are. But just don't expect everyone to react with their heads leading their hearts." Barclay knew exactly what she meant. "Thanks Dear. I should be home in good time for dinner."

It was what Faith didn't say that was important to Barclay. He had heard between the lines exactly what he needed to hear! She obviously agreed with the approach he had taken with Harry. He hadn't lost his cool, nor had he come across as one of those religious fanatics people so often associate with devout Christians. Barclay could tolerate those who disagreed with him. Reasoned arguments were his forte. But he feared encounters where emotion clouded the mind, and when one's religious hobbyhorse bucked only in one fashion.

"Hello Jane. Is Jim in?" Barclay and Jim Adams, the rector at St. Timothy's, were very close. Jane, the office secretary, often shielded incoming calls for Jim, as any good church secretary has learned to do. Jane instantly recognized Barclay's voice. "He is here, Canon. I'll put you through to him." "Hello Brother." boomed Jim's voice over the line. "What are you trying to do, out sting Harry Sting? I've got to hand it to you. That was brilliant this morning. You've done us proud!"

The two friends talked for the next ten minutes. It was good to find a personal friend one could totally trust. Jim was a wise and seasoned rector nearing the end of his career. After twenty years at St. Timothy's, he had heard and seen it all. Jim advised Barclay to listen carefully to those who would be bending his ear in the coming days.

"Don't forget." Jim said, "that those who will most violently disagree with you, are probably the most troubled in life…unsure of their own relationships with God, afraid of making a total commitment to the teachings of the church, maybe even hurt by church people somewhere along the way. Ministry, Barclay…cure of souls. I don't have to tell you that those who protest the loudest probably are hurting the most. And Barclay, I'll be interested in hearing whether your attendance at worship next Sunday is up or down."

Somehow Barclay expected it to be up. It had been a much-needed ten minutes with Jim over the phone. Jim hadn't really told him anything he didn't already know. "Just listen, Barclay, just listen." This would be his strategy as he prepared to work through the remaining pile of calls to be made.

"Might as well begin with Bill Stern," Barclay thought to himself. Bill Stern, a prominent lawyer in town and the people's warden at St. Bartholomew's, was highly respected in Tangleville. There was no question of Bill's loyalty to the parish. But Bill tended to conduct business in the church as if every matter was a legal brief. Bill and Barclay had crossed swords many a time in the past. Whenever someone in the parish wanted to get the rector's ear and didn't want to face Barclay, you could almost predict it would be through Bill Stern. And Bill would get legalistic with the rector, prepared to lay down the law on the parishioner's behalf, all in confidence with no names used, of course. "So, what could it be this time?" Barclay chuckled to himself. "You can bet I'll soon find out."

Barclay was put on hold by Bill's secretary, who told him that Mr. Stern was on the other line. Barclay said he'd wait. The cup of green tea at the upper right-hand corner of his writing pad was growing cold. "A metaphor of Bill's way with people," thought Barclay. "Why is it that some people are perceived to be so distant? So crusty? So reluctant to put others in their presence at ease?"

Barclay had thought about that a lot over the years. All the standard psychological explanations were ticking through his mind as he waited for Bill to pick up the line. Maybe, beneath that cold, professional veneer, Bill was an insecure man wearing the mask of professionalism, a cover-up for his own lack of self-worth. Maybe he was just stressed out, a candidate for burnout who hated his job and was just counting off the days until retirement. Maybe he just didn't know how to let down his guard and be truly open and at ease with people.

Perhaps the church should be offering workshops for people who want to learn how to try on another "hat," so to speak, in order to make themselves into the kind of people they would secretly like to be but are afraid to start again after so many years of living a perfected persona. Bill Stern could be any one of a thousand people in Tangleville who are hiding something they have internally loathed for years and are afraid to do anything about it, Barclay thought. Barclay knew that the two would have to talk about it, if Bill could only come to the point where his proud personality would permit it.

"Bill Stern speaking!" The professional voice was measured and aloof. "Bill, it's Barclay from the parish. How's your day going?" Barclay knew that such an opening line would give Bill a chance, if he would take it, to crack the lawyer's facade and simply talk as a friendly warden with one's rector. But wasn't about to work.

"Canon Steadmore, you've got a problem! One of our prominent members of the parish called me this morning following your stint on The Harry Sting Show and felt that you really blew it. You didn't talk about the Bible, or use enough Biblical language in your conversation with Mr. Sting. You didn't project the proper image of a clergyman. You were too philosophical in your answers. She is so upset she is threatening to cut back in her offerings at St. Bart's. What are you going to do about it?"

Barclay had heard those kinds of threats many a time in the past... the offering envelope used as blackmail.

"Did you listen to the show yourself this morning Bill?"

"Didn't have time to, Rector. I've got a law practice to run...not like some people who have the luxury of being able to knock off and be radio personalities."

Barclay wasn't about to bite Bill's baited hook about clergy flexibility when it comes to day-to-day timetabling. "Tell you what, Bill. I'll let you, as a trusted friend, in on a little secret. Next week's program is going to be tailor-made for her. So tell her that you've spoken with me and I've promised that I'll change my approach, and that she'll like it."

Barclay knew that Bill would just love to inform that unidentified parishioner that he'd solved her problem. Bill would look like he'd been effective as a rector's warden, and the tempest in a teapot would be squelched.

Father Jim at St. Timothy's was indeed a wise man. "Listen," he had advised. "Just listen." Barclay knew that it was important for Bill to be heard, and that he could tell the parishioner that she had been heard. Nothing in his plans would need to be changed as far as the next Harry Sting Show was concerned. But he had defused a potentially explosive situation by letting Bill be Bill. One of these days he'd find out really what was beneath Bill's prickly personal demeanor. "The time will come," thought Barclay. "I'll just keep listening. And I think I know who that parishioner Bill is referring to is. At least, I think I know."

Hannah Fisher was standing before Barclay's desk, a knowing smile on her face. "Looks like you just put out another fire." she quipped. "Why don't you let me top up your cup with some fresh tea before you tackle the rest of that pile of calls?"

It was late into the day before Barclay left the office. He turned the ignition key of his Jeep Liberty and welcomed the short drive to the rectory. The events of the day surged through his mind as he merged through the easy traffic to Comfort Drive. Hannah's choice of words had certainly been prophetic earlier that morning when she greeted him and said, "Tangleville had been aroused!"

"Times change," Barclay thought to himself. "But if there is anything more permanent than human nature, I certainly would like to discover it. No wonder conversion, that great theme of our Lord's Gospel, is such a needed and welcomed miracle in the lives of humankind."

He realized that Bill Bilker had not called. "Guess it all will have to wait for another day," Barclay sighed. "He'll call. If he doesn't, Sarah surely will!"

Chapter Five

THE remainder of the week would turn out to be a hectic one for Barclay...anything but a scheduled turn of events. A priest's timetable is never predictable, and certainly never routine. Like most clerics, Barclay always attempted to lay out in advance his major obligations for the coming week by penciling in major monthly and yearly fixed commitments to parish life. He tried to adhere to what he called "blocks of time," each week with segments set aside for sermon preparation, hospital, nursing home, and home visits, parish council meetings, church administration duties, and staff meetings.

Some duties were always sheer drudgery, at least for Barclay. If he could have his pick, sermon preparation and writing came at the top of his list. The academic part of preparing for the weekly homily was sheer joy. At the bottom of the list were letter writing, preparing reports for the Bishop's office, and the monthly newsletter. They were just plain hard work...routine, mundane, and never inspiring. Barclay could never understand it when fellow clergy would tell him how they spent hours in front of their computers each day. Somehow, he suspected that it was all an avoidance tactic to get out of one-on-one contact with people. "People must come first," Barclay always said. "Ministry is about touching the lives of people and meeting them where they are on a day-to-day basis."

Friday afternoon had finally arrived. Next Monday would bring him back to radio station AM KNOW, behind the microphone and across the desk from Harry Sting. Somehow, the thought of that impending show both excited and intimidated Barclay. He knew that most of his parishioners would be listening. So would the vast majority of his fellow clergy in Tangleville.

But the part that bothered him the most, even though he would never admit it to anyone else except perhaps to his loving wife Faith, was that he really wasn't sure how much support he was receiving from the clergy of Tangleville. He knew where Jim Adams' loyalty stood. But after spending so many years in ordained ministry he had learned more than he cared to know about the one-upmanship amongst the professional clergy. So many clergy seemed to emerge into a competitive move when it came to showing the Good News of the Gospels. Instead of rejoicing in each others' successes in introducing people to the joys of participation in the Kingdom of Heaven, often fellow clergy seemed to become guardians of their own fiefdoms, taking great delight when a family transferred out of a neighborhood parish and came to theirs, bragging about how much their weekly offerings have increased, or delighting in telling how many attended worship the previous Sunday. Of course, if those numbers were down from the previous year, or things were getting a little prickly in the parish, one would never hear about such negative news.

Barclay could never understand how ministry could descend to such a competitive level. After all, the church does not belong to the clergy, or even to the laity. The Church is God's gift to the world…the community of believers where everyone celebrates together over each other's successes and offers support in times of difficulty.

But Barclay was a realist. He knew that after that first AM KNOW interview with Harry Sting every minister in the town would be listening come Monday morning. There would be those clergy and laity who were just waiting for Barclay to put Harry in his place...to make Harry Sting look foolish... and see that as a triumph of the Christian faith over secularism. Barclay understood where they were coming from. The good folks were looking for a Moses to lead them back into the promised land of the past, where the church was looked upon with admiration, respectability, and prestige. Back to a time perhaps closer to the 1950s when everything seemed simpler, issues and ready answers to life's problems could be given with assurance and certitude.

Then there were those who were just waiting for Barclay to make a fool of himself over the airwaves. Some of the clergy from competitive denominations...and oh, how Barclay hated that concept of competition between churches...were hoping that he would blow it so badly that parishioners would leave St Bartholomew's and perhaps wander into one of their congregational settings. They would never admit it, of course, but jealousy was lurking just below the surface and instead of supporting Barclay in his risky verbal sparring with Harry Sting, they secretly wished that they themselves were wearing his clerical collar... the brave David taking on the secular Goliath in Tangleville, slinging words instead of round stones to slay the giant, who, week after week, seemed to take great delight in poking holes in the Christian faith.

But Barclay also knew that Harry Sting's faithful audience attracted an assortment of secularists, ranging from agnostics, New Agers, people who have become disenchanted or even hurt by the Church, to the just plain curious and all the way to out-and-out atheists, whose greatest hope is that the Church can be finally crucified and buried.

Barclay wrestled all week as to why and who he was in being involved at all with The Harry Sting Show. After all, there was more than enough for him to do in the parish without taking Monday mornings off to do Sting's show. Was he being used as a sacrificial lamb to titillate and amuse the masses? He knew, of course, that this could very well be the aim of Harry Sting. But perhaps God had opened a door for Barclay to challenge the hearts and minds of people whom he would never otherwise have had the opportunity to touch. God does work in mysterious ways. Moses, Aaron, and Mary, the mother of Jesus, and hundreds of others down through the centuries had been reluctant participants in God's revelation to the world. Perhaps even he, Barclay Steadmore, was being called upon to perform a special mission in Tangleville. Barclay was not one to say no to God.

Friday afternoon finally arrived. The sermon for Sunday was finished. Unless something was to happen somewhere in the world that was so unexpected, so relevant to his flock that he felt he needed to address the topic, then Barclay was ready for his Sunday homily. Between Friday evening and Sunday morning he might have to alter his written document. Many times in the past he felt led to scrap the main thesis of his weekly speech from the pulpit, but that was normal. He could deal with it.

He knew he could cope. After all, he'd done it many times in the past.

Chapter Six

MONDAY morning dawned sunny and bright on Comfort Drive, where the Steadmore's modest split-level home was located. There was nothing special about their residence…it was just about like everyone else's on the street. Barclay and Faith were lucky in that they had been able to purchase their own home after the parish decided to sell the rectory a few years ago and to allow future rectors a living allowance instead of providing free housing, as Anglican parishes had been doing for centuries. It would mean that, after retirement, if the two were lucky enough to live that long, they would have a little equity to begin their days on pension.

Barclay was up early that morning. After all, it was Monday, the day when he'd be back behind the microphone at station AM KNOW. The morning paper, *The People's Voice*, always arrived early on Comfort Drive. Over his first cup of coffee, before Faith was up, Barclay had already ploughed through most of the headline news. Not much seemed to have happened in Tangleville over the weekend. "No news is always welcome news," thought Barclay. But there it was in the entertainment section of the newspaper, a small advertisement for the week ahead at the radio station. Small town newspapers always have room for such local news, since advertising dollars go a long way with local publishers. And Barclay's name was there as the guest of Harry Sting, along with the caption: "Dr. Steadmore versus Harry Sting. Don't miss it!"

The old feeling of anxiety suddenly welled up within. Why was he doing this? The words "versus" almost seemed to jump from the page. All of his Christian training over the years objected to that word. Christians were to be peacemakers, not conquerors. They were to be peacemakers, not dividers, healers, not inflictors of animosity. And yet, just below the surface, Barclay sensed that very human trait of excitement of going to do battle…the thrill of possible victory. Even if he was not going to wield a sword of steel, he would be offered the opportunity to cut down the enemy with the sword of the sharp tongue. Why is the animal adversarial side of the human being so close to the surface of our veneer of civility? This bothered Barclay. One does not like to believe that human nature is so difficult to control and subdue. And the fact that the announcement appeared on the entertainment page of the paper only added salt to the wound. If there was anything a clergy person never wants to be accused of, it was of being an entertainer. Christianity is not entertainment.

"Well, Barclay, got your suit of armor polished?" Faith teased as she waited for the toast to pop. That was Faith at her best. There was always that little splash of mischief just below any conversation. Barclay loved it, and Faith knew it.

"What's the topic for the morning show?" Faith inquired.

"I don't know," Barclay answered. "That is the problem. Old Harry's too smart for that. He won't let me know in advance what he is going to hit me with. I suspect it will be controversial though. After all, he's got to be able to retain his old prickly demeanor. It keeps his ratings up, and that's the game, isn't it?"

"You sound cynical this morning, Barclay. Don't you believe in freedom of expression? He's just doing his job, isn't he? After all, it is a commercial radio station. He has to pay the bills, or there will be no AM KNOW."

"I know. I know that," replied Barclay. "But I'd like to think that Harry really believes in what he's saying…that he is genuine and not just acting. Does that make me too much of an idealist, Faith?"

The conversation between these two long-time spouses continued over breakfast. Barclay took his morning shower, shaved and dressed, and was heading out the door when Faith, as she always did whenever he left for work, gave him a little smack on the cheek and said, "Remember who you are."

The drive to station AM KNOW was uneventful. The Jeep Liberty was a delight to propel around the suburbs of Tangleville. This time Harry knew where to park, where the reception desk was located at the entrance to the station, and the routine of getting ready for the ON AIR signal.

Harry was already seated at the microphone. He even muttered "good morning" to Barclay as he was adjusting his headphones. "At least that was better than last time," thought Barclay. "At least I'm being recognized this morning. A good sign indeed."

The technician behind the control room's glass wall had raised his hand in the air. There was a slight pause. The countdown had begun… five fingers…now four…three, two, one. The ON AIR sign over the glass panel flashed on.

It was clear that Harry was at his usual best! To Barclay it seemed that his professional introduction was even more polished and eager than usual:

"Good morning, thinking people of Tangleville. You have chosen a great time to tune into this morning's edition of The Harry Sting Show because today we have the Reverend Canon Doctor Barclay Steadmore, in the hot seat once again. Steadmore is the rector of downtown St. Bartholomew's Anglican Parish, and the last time he was here, he pulled a fast one on me. He tricked me by avoiding giving an answer to my question for the topic of the day. Well, we had all kinds of feedback from you, the listening audience, on that show during the call-in section from ten thirty to eleven. This time I'm not going to beat around the bush with Steadmore. This time we'll get answers. Good morning, Doctor."

"Good morning, Mr. Sting." replied Barclay. "It is great to be back with you this morning. By the way, you don't sound very happy today. Are you okay? Do you want to talk about it?"

As soon as Barclay had uttered those words, he realized that he had once again pushed Harry into a corner. It wasn't intentional. It was simply the way a cleric would usually respond to someone who seemed to need a little pastoral care. But it was too late.

Harry's eyes narrowed as he glared at Barclay. "There you go again, Steadmore, pulling that professional caregiver shtick on me. You're not here to counsel me. You're here to answer questions this morning."

"So I'm on trial, Harry? Is that it? I thought I was to be your guest this morning. How could I have been so mistaken?" Barclay replied with a wink aimed at Harry. Of course, the radio audience wouldn't have caught that action, but already Barclay and Harry were off to playing the game of pretended animosity.

"Listen, Steadmore, let's get right down to the topic for today. The last time you were here, you pulled that 'hat trick' on me, remember? I asked you a question and you responded by saying, 'Do you want me to answer by wearing my secular hat or my sacred hat?' Well, today we're wise to you. Today I want you to answer my questions from a theological perspective by wearing your sacred hat. Got it?"

"Fire away, Harry. I'm already adjusting my clerical collar." Barclay chuckled. "What's the topic for today?"

"Lotteries and gambling…state legalized games of chance," grinned Harry from across the desk. As expected, it took Barclay completely by surprise. Harry always made it his practice to never tell clergy guests the topic of conversation before his shows. This way Harry could catch religious leaders off guard and play the devil's advocate over the airways.

"So what's the question?" responded Barclay. "What are you asking of me? That I sanction such events? That the state should have legalized such occurrences? That it is good or bad for society? You'll have to be a little more specific. Remember, you've got me 'by the collar' this morning." Harry couldn't miss the pun on the word 'collar,' as Barclay reached up and tugged at his clerical collar.

Harry grinned, but came right back with his standard professional, one-upmanship type of reply. "You know what I mean, Steadmore. Do you approve of legalized lotteries and gambling?"

"No" was Barclay's reply. Harry waited for Barclay to continue. But Barclay just sat there, smiling at Harry. Now the worst thing that can happen on a radio show is what is called 'dead air,' and the air was dead for five seconds, until Harry broke the silence.

"Well, why not?" he blurted out.

"My Christian faith doesn't allow it," replied Barclay. "I have no Biblical authority…by that I mean traditional theological permission…to do so, nor, for that matter, to sanction society to do so. Christian traditionalists have always considered such pastimes 'vice,' not 'virtuous conduct.' Nothing has changed in Christian thinking to alter the church's position on these matters. So, as a member of the clergy and a practicing Christian, what did you expect me to say? That I agree with secularism?"

"Well surely you have to admit that we live in modern times," snapped Harry. "There is such a thing as separation of church and state, you know. The church, indeed, all religions of every kind, cannot dictate to society what it can and can't do. If people want to spend their money on lotteries and casino gambling, and if both are legal, then why shouldn't they?"

"Why shouldn't they, indeed?" answered Barclay. There was another pregnant pause over the airwaves.

"But wait a minute, Steadmore. First you said you didn't approve. How can you say why shouldn't people participate? You can't have it both ways, Doctor!"

"Harry, I think a little confusion has slipped into this conversation. You asked me if I approve and I said 'no.' I also answered that as a Christian I don't approve. But if secular society is not governed or guided by a moral authority higher than that of the state, nor by one's own personal, private concept of morality, then my authority is not their authority. Why shouldn't they spend their money any way they please? I don't believe that it is the church's business to impose morality upon society. Rather, it's better to lead than to drive opinion."

"Doctor, you slipped out of that one just a little too easily. I can't let you off the hook just yet. What about the argument that the proceeds of lotteries go to support hundreds of charities…charities that do all kinds of good in society. The church is a charitable organization, so why would you object to raising money for good works?"

"No one argues against raising monies for charities. But do you honestly believe that people spend monies at the gambling venues to enrich the coffers of charitable organizations? If you believe that, you are a naïve fellow, and I don't for a minute think that of you, Harry. You and I both know that one of those seven deadly sins, the sin of 'greed' is behind the act. How can one argue that charity is one's motive for giving when personal gain is possibly involved? To say one gambles for the sake of charity is an alibi for one's inner desire to experience personal advantage. Don't you agree, Harry?"

The technician behind the glass partition was waving frantically at Harry. There were ten of his fingers in the air. Ten seconds to go before the first commercial break. Harry squeezed in his final few words:

"We'll be back folks, in two minutes. Don't go away. I'm not finished with Dr. Steadmore yet, so stay tuned."

The ON AIR light went blank.

Barclay didn't wait for Harry to begin the off-air conversation. "It's not going that well, is it Harry?" Barclay began. "That first half of the show didn't do much for your ratings. It was too predictable, too uneventful. Why don't you let me throw something into our conversation that will rile up your audience? I can guarantee you that I can still defend my Christian principles, but put another view across that non-religious people won't want to hear. What do you say?"

"I don't know if I can trust you, Barclay." replied Harry. "Why would you do that for me?"

"Because I am a Christian, Harry, You'll just have to trust me."

"Okay, what do you want me to do in the next half of the show?"

"Just ask me to take off that clerical collar and put on my secular hat and you'll find out." explained Barclay.

The technician's hand was in the air. Barclay and Harry waited for the ON AIR sign to flash on. Barclay's heart was racing. There was no denying that he was excited. Harry looked to be a little worried across the desk, but Barclay was sure that there was a rapport developing between them.

Harry began;

> "Welcome back folks to the second half of The Harry Sting Show. If you have tuned in late today, our guest is the Reverend Canon Doctor Barclay Steadmore, rector of St. Bartholomew's Anglican Church in downtown Tangleville. Today's topic is legalized lotteries and casino gambling. In the first half of the show, Doctor Steadmore was on the hot seat, and as I might have predicted, he told us he is against such activities. But after all, he's a clergyman. What else can he say, I suppose? So in this portion of the show I'm going to try something different. I'm going to see if his human nature can show through, and not his spiritually required pat answers."

Harry was actually smiling at Barclay. "So, Doctor Steadmore, let's cut through all this standard Christian propaganda and get real. I'm going to ask you to do something that I'm sure you won't want to do. I'm going to ask you to take off that clerical collar of yours and come down to earth with us mortals to answer the question from a more secular position. If your Christian morality was not your guide to your behavior, would you personally participate in lotteries and casino gambling?"

"No." replied Barclay. There was again a few seconds of dead air. For just a few seconds Barclay thought he could detect a hint of disappointment on Harry's face, then a hint of near panic. Barclay, using both hands to make a circular motion, signaled across the desk for Harry to follow up on his curt one word answer.

"Well, why not, Steadmore? If religious convictions are not your taskmaster, then why not?"

"Harry, we no longer live in a world where it is fashionable to adhere to a set of rules for moral absolutes. In our modern world today everyone is one's own theologian. That means moral freedom, which assumes that all moral choices are of equal value and equally valid. No one today can criticize one another's freedom to choose one's morality. So, if I were not a Christian, which indeed restricts my moral choices, and since you have just asked me to lose my religious shackles, my answer would still be 'no.' But my 'no' would be entirely for selfish reasons. Would you like me to explain?"

" I think you better." conceded Harry.

"Look, Harry, lotteries and casino gambling are taxes that I refuse to pay. They are voluntary taxes on those who are foolish enough to pay them. Now, look at it this way. Every thinking person knows that the state lotteries and casinos never go under. There is a built-in formula to prevent this. So the government has an instant cash cow in these matters, which generates millions of dollars every year to help balance their budgets. Now Harry, just think…the more a country can encourage its citizens to gamble, the greater its revenues…taxes which only willing participants are required to pay. Now here is why the selfish, but smart citizen can benefit by not gambling. Someone else is paying taxes for them…monies that if not raised in such a fashion would have to be raised by taxes levied on everyone. So non-gamblers should be delighted that others are paying the taxes for them. Just think, Harry. In theory, if a country could get enough people to gamble there is the possibility that all revenues, all government finances, could be raised without income taxes, gasoline taxes, and sales taxes. Why some of us wouldn't have to pay taxes at all. Wouldn't that be great?"

"That wouldn't be fair," sputtered Harry. "Why, that is taking advantage of people...people who perhaps can't afford to spend their hard-earned cash that way."

"Harry, don't get moral on me! Don't you believe in freedom of choice? In a morally neutral society, you're not required to be your sister's keeper. Why are you toying with guilt? Moral guilt is not necessary when there are no moral absolutes."

"But Steadmore, if people's gambling gets them into financial chaos, think of all the extra services society would need to provide... rehabilitation centers, counselors, lawyers for law suits, credit experts to sort out peoples' ruined lives. Think of the expenses involved."

"Now you've got it Harry. Imagine all the new extra jobs...paychecks to take home for those needed to deal with people who were in way over their heads. Don't you believe in generating new jobs, Harry? Do you gamble, Harry?"

"No, I don't," snapped Harry.

"Well then...congratulations! You're a winner when it comes to avoiding taxes. Maybe we shouldn't be telling your audience not to gamble. It disadvantages people like you and me!"

There was another pregnant pause in the show. Harry leaned back in his chair and grinned at Barclay. Both knew that it had been a great show. Harry realized that his listening audience would be more than provoked by Barclay's suggestion that gamblers were being used by the state. The show's ratings would remain sky high. And Barclay knew that he had come through with a consistent argument for living out the Christian standards of moral absolutes.

"Put the collar back on, Doctor Steadmore." smiled Harry. "Our time is almost up this morning." After the ON AIR light went out Harry leaned across the desk to shake Barclay's hand.

"I think we've got a good thing going here. Do you think you might wish to become a regular Monday guest on my show?"

Barclay took his hand and said: "I'll think about it. I'll have to ask Faith what she has to say."

"I know what you mean" Harry smiled back. "I'm married too."

CHAPTER SEVEN

BARCLAY was feeling elated as he climbed into his Jeep Liberty to head back to his office. It was a beautiful Monday morning. The sun was shining. The birds were busy building nests in the branches of the trees lining the streets of Tangleville. In Barclay's mind, the morning with Harry Sting had gone well…very well, indeed.

To be a regular guest on Harry's show would perhaps open up a ministry for Barclay that he would never be able to do otherwise. Harry had actually warmed to Barclay…at least that's the way Barclay saw it. Now the rest of the day and the week lay ahead.

Barclay's thoughts were interrupted by the sound of his cell phone. It was the church office calling:

"Barclay here." he responded. It was Hannah calling and she seemed to be a little on edge. "Dr. Steadmore, are you going to be returning to the office in the next few minutes?"

"I should be there in about fifteen minutes, Hannah. What's up?"

"Bishop Strictman is waiting for you in your office and he is not smiling." Hannah said. "He arrived about forty-five minutes ago and listened to your interview with Harry Sting on your office radio. My guess is he's somewhat concerned." Barclay knew that Hannah had a way with words. "Somewhat concerned" was code for an upset bishop.

"Put on the tea, Hannah. And make it strong," teased Barclay. " I'll be there as soon as I can."

Barclay's mind was racing as he pulled into the church parking lot. Bishop Strictman had a habit of dropping into parishes unannounced. So today's visit was not out of the ordinary. But what was the meaning of Hannah's statement "somewhat concerned?" Had he forgotten to send some report to the synod office? Was St. Bartholomew's behind in its monthly apportionment of monies sent each month to the central office to help run the diocese? Could it be that there might be disapproval of his involvement at station AM KNOW? Well, there was only one way to find out, thought Barclay.

As Barclay rushed through the outer office where Hannah professionally controlled the day-to-day activities of the parish office, he couldn't help but notice a little smile on her face. "The Bishop is much more relaxed now." she whispered, "and he's ready for a second cup of tea. I'll take yours in a few minutes after you two get settled."

Bishop Strictman was a man in his late fifties with a large frame and a sincere, very much in command demeanor; he was a no-nonsense, very orthodox, fatherly bishop, not only to his priests and deacons, but also to everyone who fell under his episcopal jurisdiction. Barclay and Bishop Strictman were close friends and it was evident to everyone in the diocese that these two loved and respected each other. However, Barclay was under no illusion that they were equals. Bishop Strictman was his superior and both the Bishop and Barclay knew it. If there was one thing that was never in doubt, it was that Bishop Strictman was a skilled, conservative theologian, one who was always fair and confidential in his dealings with clergy and individuals. Everyone knew what he stood for and where he stood theologically. However, everyone under his jurisdiction also knew that he did not like surprises. If one was to present an issue, a new venture, an experimental concept with him, he always listened carefully and usually granted his blessing to proceed. Just keep him informed. Barclay was of the same mindset. Perhaps that is why he and the Bishop got along so famously.

"Good morning, Bishop." Barclay smiled as he reached out to grasp his superior's hand. Bishop Strictman rose to accept Barclay's gesture as they embraced one another. "Good morning, Canon."

The door to the church office was still open as Barclay waited for Hannah to make her entrance with the tray of tea. In public, Barclay and the Bishop always presented a formal approach for others to observe. But behind closed doors, in private situations, it was a matter of custom to call each other by first names.

The tea arrived and upon leaving Hannah closed the door to the rector's office. The two old friends settled down to continue their meeting. Barclay was relieved that the Bishop didn't seem too upset, at least not the way Hannah had first described over the phone.

They exchanged niceties, each asking about spouses and children and each other's health. The pressures of ministry, both knew, could take its toll on dedicated clergy.

"Barclay, I'm here because I received a letter from Bill Stern last week."

"George, I bet I know what it's all about," Barclay responded. "He's a little ticked off that I am involved with The Harry Sting Show. Am I right?"

"You got it, Barclay. The letter took me by surprise, as I didn't know you were going to be interviewed. However, that matter aside, Bill made it sound like you were doing a disservice to the parish. Here's his letter. You'd better read it."

Barclay leaned forward to receive the envelope from the bishop's hand, opened it, and began to scan the page…a one-page letter written on Bill's law office stationery.

My Dear Bishop Strictman:

As a warden of St. Bartholomew's parish, I feel it is my duty to inform you that my rector, the Reverend Canon Doctor Barclay Steadmore, has overstepped his parish mandate.

Recently he has been a guest on The Harry Sting Show, at station AM KNOW…a morning one-hour program designed, in my opinion, to titillate the chattering classes. Mr. Sting has focused on matters trivializing religion and faith. I am concerned that Canon Steadmore is rather naïve and will be used by Mr. Sting to further the ratings of his show. I have spoken over the telephone with Canon Steadmore following the show, expressing my displeasure with his activities. Canon Steadmore refused to take my complaint seriously and gave me no assurance that this is the end of the matter. I only have the best interest of St. Bartholomew's in mind as I now refer this concern to your attention.

I look forward to your reply!

Sincerely,

Mr. William J. Stern

Crabpear, McTrust and Stern

Barristers and Solicitors

Bishop Strictman was leaning back in his chair savouring the last of his second cup of tea as Barclay folded the letter and passed it back to his superior.

"Bill has a way with words, doesn't he George?"

"That is why I am here today, Barclay. I just had to check it out with you. But after listening to part of the show this morning, I think Bill has rather misjudged what you are trying to do for the church and the general public who tune in each week. I was very impressed with how you handled the topic from both sides of the fence…from the sacred and the secular. There is no doubt about it…your message was consistent and sound. Perhaps a bit rough on secular society, but very honest indeed."

Barclay sighed a silent breath of relief. Now to tell his Bishop that he was considering accepting a weekly guest invitation to join Mr. Sting.

"George, thank you for your endorsement. I had no idea how many people in Tangleville listened to Mr. Sting's program. Everywhere I went last week people came up to me to tell me how much they agreed or disagreed with my comments. Even other clergy called the office. There were two new families in the pews yesterday following last week's show."

"Let me ask, Barclay…were you not afraid of being used by Mr. Sting? Television, radio, and show business can be seductive, you know."

This was Barclay's chance to break the news to his Bishop. "At first I was, but I've come to realize that Mr. Sting is not the individual he appears to present over the airwaves. He has invited me to be a regular guest on his show. I'm going to accept his invitation simply because I feel I can use the exposure to spread the Good News of the faith. At the same time, I'm convinced that Harry is willing to readily allow me to present the message of the Gospel. Of course, he has to play the devil's advocate to keep up his ratings."

Bishop Strictman cast a sly smile toward Barclay. "Canon, I know I'm being manipulated this morning, but I'm all for trying any avenue that introduces Christ to the masses. You've got my permission to accept Sting's invitation, with one proviso. Send me a monthly report of the topics you have discussed on the show and give me your word that if things are getting out of hand you'll cease your electronic ministry."

"A deal, Bishop. But what about Bill Stern?"

"I'll handle it." grinned the Bishop. "Leave him to me!"

There was no question in Barclay's mind that, indeed, Bishop Strictman would deal with Bill Stern. Now to wait and see how Bill Stern would deal with his rector.

Bishop Strictman shook hands with Barclay, told him to give his personal greetings to Faith, and walked to the outer office and complimented Hannah on her tea making abilities. In seconds he was gone and Hannah and Barclay stood there smiling at each other.

"Well, Doctor, have you still got a job!" she teased.

"It was your crumpets and tea that did it." grinned Barclay. Both knew that another potential fire in the parish had been extinguished… at least for now.

CHAPTER EIGHT

IT had been quite a week following last Monday's radio show with Harry…the one where he and Harry had debated the merits of legalized gambling. Harry had called Barclay the following Wednesday afternoon to tell him that the station had been inundated with telephone calls and emails from listeners. There was almost an even split between those who agreed with Barclay calling gambling a "cash cow" for governments and those who were extremely upset by his statements that he hoped more people would be enticed to throw the dice so the non-gamblers could get out of paying more taxes. Harry was on cloud nine with the ratings…after all, ratings are everything in radio and television.

Barclay knew that Harry really wasn't too concerned about the morality of gambling…at least that is what he suspected was the case. But Barclay was coming from a completely different perspective than that of Harry. Barclay wanted the moral argument to be the dominant reason for the listeners not to gamble. At the moment, both were in a 'win-win' situation. Harry's ratings were soaring and Barclay was using the show to teach Christian principles to the listening audience. For the time being, both could live with the situation.

Barclay was more than encouraged that Bishop Strictman was onside. And so was Faith. After Bishop Strictman's visit to his office last Monday, that evening Faith and Barclay had had a long conversation regarding Harry's invitation to be a weekly guest on the show. As usual, Faith made some logical arguments for her husband to be leery of the entire coming arrangement. Faith was concerned that he would end up being manipulated by Harry and that in the process of doing a weekly show Barclay would become a celebrity figure for all the wrong reasons. Was it really the "Good News" that Barclay was promoting? Was it a matter of pride, just below the surface, where Barclay, who sometimes loved to argue just for the sheer sake of intellectual stimulation, would tangle with Harry and sense the possibility of winning? That would be wrong, she insisted. Pride is such a subtle sin, sweet to the senses, yet always setting one up for a potential fall.

A compromise was reached between the two. They agreed that Barclay should give it a go for two months and that Faith and he would then re-evaluate the situation. In the meantime, Faith would listen to each program and keep notes on the proceedings. Barclay was feeling elated by their decision.

Now Barclay was more relaxed than usual as he drove to the radio station for the following Monday's show. It had been a great relief that both Faith and Bishop Strictman had given their blessings to his new weekly experiment in ministry. This was the first show that wouldn't be a surprise to him. Harry had always refused in the past to tell Barclay the topic to be discussed over the air. But after he and Harry had agreed to work together, Harry had called Barclay during the middle of the previous week to announce the theme of the show for the coming Monday. Harry wanted to address the concept of absolute right and wrong in an evolving pluralistic society. Barclay was delighted with the topic. Of course, he was not sure how Harry was going to steer the on-air conversation, but at least he had a general idea of the concept of the task ahead. Harry, Barclay was certain, would take the position that in a secular society, moral absolutes were no longer possible, nor, indeed, desirable. It promised to be a great opportunity for debate.

For Harry, it was a much more relaxed preparation for the ten o'clock show than in the past. Harry had met Barclay in the waiting room and both shared a few minutes of civilized conversation over coffee. Together they walked into the control room and prepared for the red ON AIR light to flash. A few minutes early, Harry smiled from across his desk, the big structure which separated himself from his weekly guests, and asked Barclay the question: "Ready Canon?" Barclay mentally noted that Harry was calling him by his correct title: Canon. Harry must have done some research into what the title means and was now willing to use it on the air. "Are we going to give our listening audience a good show this morning?"

Barclay didn't respond as he wanted to. For him this wasn't a show, a time for entertainment. This was a deadly serious occasion…an opportunity for folks out there to be confronted with spiritual ideas that may cause them to become aware of God's demands upon their lives, perhaps for the first time. But Barclay, biting his tongue, smiled and replied, "Let's give it a go! I'm excited this morning to be with you. Are we agreeing to disagree, as usual, on this next half hour?"

"You've got it, Canon. We must appear to be at odds with one another or we'll lose the opportunity to stir up the audience." Barclay winced at Harry's statement.

The ON AIR sign flashed on and Harry began his opening monologue.

> *"Good Morning, thinking people of Tangleville. I'm glad*
> *you are with me today on The Harry Sting Show. Canon*

Doctor Steadmore, Rector of St. Bartholomew's Parish, is back in the hot seat. You are going to hear a lot more from this local priest in the upcoming weeks. He has agreed to be a regular on each Monday's program. This will give you, informed people of Tangleville, an opportunity to call in during the second half of the show to express your opinions about topics he and I will debate. Steadmore is, in my opinion, out of touch with the values of today's enlightened society. But you judge for yourself."

"Good morning Canon. Welcome. Are you ready to defend your archaic views this morning?" As Harry spoke those words, he smiled across the desk at Barclay. If only the audience could sense the show business side of talk radio. But, as Barclay well knew, it was Harry's bread and butter livelihood. After all, he was only trying to make a living…and, of course, a name for himself.

"Let's go for it Harry. What's the topic for today?" Barclay had agreed that all on air shows would appear to the listening audience to be spontaneous, that he as a guest would appear to be learning of the day's topic for the day while on air. Harry didn't want the audience to know that he and Barclay had prepared themselves in advance. Barclay didn't feel entirely comfortable with this ruse. But he had reluctantly agreed to play along. Was this his first seduction to fame in show business, he thought to himself. "Time will tell. I can handle it," he thought.

Harry, with his prepared script before him, replied. "Religion is out of date in the 21st century, isn't it, Canon? Religion insists upon moral absolutes. But you and I both know there are no absolutes in this world. Everything is evolving. Nothing stays the same. Aren't you religious types preaching into the wind?"

"Ah, so that is where Harry was going," Barclay thought to himself. "The old adage that religious moral values were obsolete. Changelessness in life is a myth."

"Harry, I am assuming that you are implying that there are no absolutes in life. But, what about death and taxes?" Barclay teased.

Harry frowned from across the desk. Never losing a beat, he came back with the words: "Canon, quit playing games. You know what I mean."

"But Harry, you said everything is evolving; nothing stays the same. I'm only trying to make a point here for the sake of clarification. 'Nothing' is a big field of investigation. What about mathematical truth? There are only three authorities for proving two triangles congruent. Two sides and a contained angle equal...two angles and a contained side equal... three equal corresponding sides. These laws have not changed from the beginning..."

"Stop right there, Canon," interrupted Harry. "You've made your point. That's not what I mean and you know it. I'm talking about moral truth. About rules that in the past guided the actions of societies...religious controls, absolute standards of right and wrong. Of all people, you as a priest ought to admit how times have changed."

"They certainly have Harry, for some people. No question about it. We live in a society that delights in inventing standards as we go. Notice, I said 'for some people....'"

"And who are they, Canon?"

"People who invent their own authority base for establishing them," replied Barclay. "But there are millions of people in this world who claim we don't have that power, that authority, to invent fixed moral precepts. Only God has that power. We can reject them or accept them... that is our choice, of course. But in so doing we don't change divine revelation. We just reap the rewards of obedience, or suffer the consequences of discarding them."

"But times are changing, Canon. You can't deny it. Just take the way people are living together before marriage, premarital sexual relationships, abortion, legalized gambling, mercy killings, etcetera, etcetera, etcetera…all these are tolerated, even accepted, in our society. All these examples of moral behavior would not have been tolerated a few decades ago. Now they are. What happened to moral absolutes?"

"Nothing," replied Barclay as he smiled across the desk at Harry. There was a long pause…dead air…and Barclay just waited for Harry to respond.

"Nothing? What do you mean nothing?" snapped Harry.

"I mean nothing has happened to moral absolutes, to divine authority. God has not changed His mind. Society has simply decided to discard the authority of religion and rewrite the script. The real question is whether or not we can call the new authority base 'truth.' What do you think Harry?"

"Sure we can! All those examples of society's moral choices exist. They are real. Sure it's truth!"

"But what if these standards change in the future? They certainly have changed from the past. They most likely will in the future. So, Harry, is your concept of 'the truth' a flexible one? Truth for the moment? Evolving truth? Maybe in mathematics we'll pronounce a fourth authority for claiming two triangles congruent. I can hardly wait."

"Ouch," thought Barclay. That last sentence was just a little too sarcastic to suit the occasion. It was all true, of course, but there was really no need for such a sledgehammer blow when perhaps a tack hammer would have driven home the point. Faith would be surely taking notes as she listened to the program.

Barclay was certain that Harry was struggling to reply, so Barclay decided to continue without waiting for Harry to respond. "Harry, I think what you're getting at is that society's base for making moral choices is not as rigid, not as fixed or as universally agreed upon as it once was. Am I right?"

"That is what I'm trying to get across Barclay. This is not the same culture in which you and I grew up. We now live in a pluralistic society. It is no longer predominately Christian. The church has no place any longer dictating to the state. Separation of church and state, my good friend, is the only way to go, and you know it."

Harry held up his two hands with extended fingers to signal that a break was coming in ten seconds, then continued. "We have to break now for two minutes. Don't go away, I can't wait to hear what Doctor Steadmore has to say."

The ON AIR sign went out and both Harry and Barclay leaned back in their chairs as they waited for the commercials to pass. "Barclay, how are we doing?" Harry smiled over his desk at his on-air opponent.

"I'm not sure that we're there yet, Harry," Barclay replied. "In the second half I'll try and clarify my position for you. I think we've introduced some fuzzy 21st century concepts that need further explanation on my part. But it sure is a timely topic you've picked. I think I need this coffee cup refilled."

Someone in the control room must have heard Barclay's request for a refill, and it wasn't long before an assistant rushed in with a new cup of freshly brewed dark roast, Barclay's favorite. After a few more seconds of pleasant banter, the man in the control room was signaling to Harry that the ten-second countdown to airtime had begun.

The ON AIR sign flashed and Harry began his intro for the second half of the show that he was sharing with Barclay.

"Welcome back folks to the second half of The Harry Sting Show. My guest this morning is the Reverend Canon Doctor Barclay Steadmore, rector of St. Bartholomew's Anglican Church here in Tangleville, and the topic for today is…."

The second half of the show differed little from the first section. It was clear that neither Harry nor Barclay were prepared to concede points to one another. Neither one was convincing the other of the merits of their arguments. But it soon became apparent to Barclay that if either one of them were to admit on air that the other was making progress then the show would be a failure of a sort. After all, it was the audience that really mattered. To stir them up was Harry's aim, but to convey spiritual truths was the desire of Barclay. In reality they were truly on opposite sides of the issue in more ways than one. Harry had ratings to worry about and Barclay knew that he had no choice but to be faithful to his religious convictions.

"Was this radio show," Barclay thought to himself, "just a modern updating of the times?" Jesus debated with the opposition of His day, with the rich young man who wanted to know what he must do to find salvation, or the time when Pilate asked Jesus, "What is truth?" Barclay was painfully aware that Jesus made converts to the Kingdom of Heaven through His personal attention to the needs of His followers…healing the sick, casting out demons, feeding the hungry, or personal intervention rather than the brute force of argumentation… love in action.

Yet, it was such fun to do the show with Harry. There were advantages, clear advantages, in being there every Monday on the air with Harry. Attendance at St. Bartholomew's Sunday services was certainly increasing. Barclay couldn't walk down the streets of Tangleville without someone congratulating him for putting Harry in his place on the show. Barclay's ego was certainly being stroked and it felt good. Celebrity status clearly had its benefits. But was God the recipient of Barclay's new-found notoriety? For now, Barclay would try to put those thoughts in the parking lot of his being. If he was to get out of control, he was sure he could deal with it. And Faith would certainly keep him humble and on track.

CHAPTER NINE

TUESDAY was broken up by hospital visits, two hours spent in his office with long-time parishioners who needed to nail down final dates and details of the upcoming annual church bazaar, and a number of telephone calls from outright strangers who wanted to debate his position taken with Harry Sting. Wednesday morning had rolled around much more quickly than usual, it seemed. Barclay was still reflecting on the previous Monday's radio show, going over and over in his mind the contents of the time spent on air.

Hannah had somehow not been able to screen out the intent of these callers and had passed them through to Barclay. Every caller had ended up giving Barclay an earful of reasons why he had been totally out of touch with modern society during the show. "What a waste of my time," Barclay concluded at the end of the sixth such call. "Here I am at the end of Wednesday and I still haven't touched the readings for next Sunday, let alone settle on the final contents of the bulletin for the coming week. This will put Hannah behind an entire day in her busy secretarial schedule."

As his mind reflected on the duties of his role as rector at the parish, doubt, and even a few pangs of guilt, were beginning to surface. What was happening in his life? Who was he becoming? What were the real priorities of a parish rector? Was he beginning to be seduced by a growing love affair with fame and recognition in the city? Was he spending the same amount of time as before The Harry Sting Show in the preparation of his weekly sermon and time spent counseling in his office with his parish flock?

It seemed strange that Bill Bilker had not called him. Sarah had seemed so distressed that day at the take-out window a few weeks ago. Were they still together? Was her cry for help that morning real, or was she simply going to put up with Bill's threats of violence? How much longer should he as rector let these questions linger before he should take the initiative and intervene? "Maybe next week." thought Barclay. "I really don't have the time to do so right now. Besides, Harry's topic for next Monday needed much more thought. I'll get around to Bill and Sarah in due course."

Hannah's voice on the office intercom broke up Barclay's inner musings. "Barclay, Harry Sting in on the line. Are you available to take his call?"

"Put him on Hannah. Let's see what he's up to now."

"Good morning Harry. What can I do for you?"

"Barclay, I won't take up much of your time this morning. I know that you are a busy man. You must be spending time, I hope, in going over your position on the topic for next Monday's show…the 'Marshmallow Church,' remember? It should be good for lots of reaction from the public. And by the way, Barclay, can you and Faith come over this coming Sunday evening for dinner? We'll have to make it late in the evening…wait until it gets quite dark. I don't want people to see you parking in the driveway in full view of the neighbors. Don't wear your clerical collar. People might recognize you. After all, I have a reputation to protect. I can't let the world see us two together. What would they think? It could be destructive to the trust my listening audience has in me. Can't risk that, can I, Canon?"

Barclay was so taken aback by Harry's words and invitation that he really needed more time to think it through. What was Harry up to? Harry had a reputation to protect. What about his own reputation? Did that not matter? Who was being the hypocrite in all of this, anyway?

Barclay stalled for time and said, "Let me check my schedule and see what I've got on Sunday evening, Harry. On his Blackberry he could see that Sunday evening was totally blank. Wouldn't he know it? There was a long, pregnant pause as Barclay wrestled with an excuse to provide him with a plausible "no" to the invitation. Finally he said, "Faith and I have plans for Sunday night, Harry. We'll have to set another date sometime in the future." Surely Harry would catch on to the word 'sometime.'

But Harry didn't give up easily. "Can we set another date now to get together?"

"Harry, I've got another call coming through. Let me get back to you in a day or two."

The other call coming through was from Hannah who in her professional way had sensed that she needed to intervene to provide the excuse Barclay needed to get out of an extended conversation, one he really needed to be rescued from at the moment. Hannah was a pro…a lifesaver many times over in the past. She was worth every dollar the parish paid her monthly, a meagre salary to say the least.

"Canon, please get back soon, it's urgent," Harry said. "We'll talk then. And thanks!"

Barclay was simply astonished by Harry's call. He walked into Hannah's office next door and found halting words to thank her for rescuing him from Harry. Then he returned to his office, picked up the telephone, and called home. He and Faith needed to talk. Something had to be worked out for Sunday evening so the two of them could validate the excuse he had given to Harry. The phone rang six times and went into voice mail mode. "Faith, call me as soon as possible. Love ya!"

The rest of the day was a bit of a bewildering one for Barclay. He tried to juggle the urgent plans for the rest of the week, all the while fretting over Harry's call. He managed to outline a rough copy of the upcoming Sunday bulletin for Hannah to type and dashed off six letters that needed to be drafted to various parishioners…cards of congratulations in recognition of anniversary events, birthday wishes and replies to correspondence he had received over the past week, letters that really were now overdue. There didn't seem to be enough time in the day to deal with his never-ending administrative duties. He, like so many other clergy, found coping with the administrative duties of the parish to be on the bottom rung of priestly satisfaction.

Just before four thirty the telephone rang. Hannah passed it on to Barclay. "It's Faith, Doctor."

"Faith, what would you love to do this coming Sunday evening? Let's get out of the house, just the two of us and spend some time together." Barclay waited for her reply.

"Don't you remember?" she asked. "We have tickets to the symphony. How could you forget?"

Barclay hung up the telephone and breathed a sigh of relief. He hadn't actually lied to Harry after all. Saved by the grace of God!

CHAPTER TEN

BARCLAY could hardly wait for Wednesday to pass at the office. He needed to sit down over dinner with Faith and bring her up to date on Harry's call that morning inviting them both for a late evening dinner together. Faith was exactly the one to help him cut through some of the questions surrounding the call. After years of marriage, it was always Faith who could offer insight into situations that he struggled over. Whereas he prided himself in his rational powers to solve problems, Faith was the one who possessed intuitive insight into solutions that he could not even conceive were possible. Many times he had jokingly accused her of possessing psychic powers. She'd laugh and respond by saying, "It is so obvious. Where have you been all your life? We women can't be fooled by mere facades." And many times her hunches had proven to be spot on.

Over his favorite dessert...blueberry pie and coffee...Barclay related to Faith the details of Harry's invitation. He confessed to her that he had to stall in accepting the invitation, even admitting that he felt that he had lied when he told Harry that something else was planned for the coming Sunday evening. He admitted as well that he had forgotten that he and Faith had tickets for the symphony in town.

There was laughter when Faith smiled that coy smile of hers and said, "I knew it. You didn't record it in your cellphone when I told you I'd picked up the tickets last week. Didn't you check my e-mail this morning when I sent you the reminder that we were going?"

Barclay was guilty of not remembering. "Maybe that's why," he thought to himself, "that when he told Harry that Sunday evening was already taken, deep down in the depths of his unconscious memory bank he felt that Sunday evening was out of the question." Not likely, but somehow it helped him appease his guilty soul for at least coming close to deception…a tiny, tiny white lie. There is a real question for Harry's program, he thought to himself: "When is a lie not a lie?"

Faith broke up his side-tracked concentration interval by saying, "I'll bet he's got a problem that he's ready to share with someone he trusts." Barclay had already got that far in his thinking.

"But what kind of a problem could it be?" he asked her.

"Well," she responded, "I'll put my money on the table that it has something to do with guilt and he needs to deal with the matter. You, Barclay, are about to hear a confession."

"Guilt! The man doesn't even have that word in his vocabulary," Barclay responded.

"Yes he does." Faith replied. "I've thought for some time now that Harry is a very unhappy individual. I think that he's about to become a new man."

"Well then, shall we go? Shall I set a date with him? When will it work for you?"

Faith responded that the Sunday following next would work just fine. "It will give me time to go shopping for something to wear," she grinned. "I've never met his wife, so I've just got to be presentable."

"I'll call Harry first thing tomorrow morning," Barclay responded. "I'd really like another piece of that blueberry pie!"

They sat in silence for a few minutes. Barclay finished his second piece of pie, which he knew he really didn't need given his constant battle with a threatening waistline. Faith proceeded to clear the table and after pouring him his third cup of coffee realized that something was taking shape in his mind. "What's the matter?" You are wrestling with something, aren't you?"

"Maybe I should call Harry right now and see if he's able to receive us a week from Sunday. Maybe I shouldn't wait until morning to return his call."

"Look, Doctor." She always used the title "Doctor" when she was trying to help him avoid a mistake in his life. "Don't call him at home whatever you do. Suppose his spouse answers. And suppose she doesn't know a thing about what Harry is planning for the get-together. Maybe he hasn't told her a word about the potential night. Maybe it was just a spur of the moment request of his for us to come. You are the professional. Do it the way it should be handled. Call him tomorrow, late in the afternoon after his daily show is over. And whatever you do, let Hannah put the call through for you. Don't give him the idea that you are concerned about the visit. You need to convey to him that you are busy and have found a way to work him into your schedule. After all, he needs to know that your parish obligations are first in your busy life."

"Faith, you are right. How was I able to pick out such a smart wife all those years ago?"

"What do you mean you picked me?" Maybe I picked you," she grinned. Barclay knew it was not the time to go there.

They watched the news together, walked hand in hand to the bedroom, said their prayers, kissed goodnight, and told each other that they loved one another.

Just before Barclay fell asleep he thought to himself, "Strange how God can bring two very different people together who complement one another in so many ways. The institution of marriage sure is a mystery."

CHAPTER ELEVEN

THE rest of the week had passed pretty much like all others. Thursday and Friday were days in preparation for the coming homily for Sunday. Hannah was rushing around the office trying to tie up details for the week preparing the Sunday bulletin, answering the office phone, sending emails to parishioners who hadn't been out to worship over the past three weeks to enquire if they were ill or if they needed a clergy visit, and to generally keep in touch in case there were problems that should be passed on to the rector.

Saturday was to be a heavy day…a funeral in the morning and a wedding in the afternoon. He knew that come nine o'clock Saturday evening he would be physically wiped. To go from the emotional lows of a funeral in the morning, sharing in the grief of the distraught family members, to suddenly having to put on a smiling demeanor and portray the happiness and joy of a wedding ceremony was not easy. Life and death, sorrow and joy are the building blocks of reality.

The funeral was for long-time member of St. Bartholomew's choir, Janet Robinson, and would take place at ten in the morning; the wedding of Jill Hudson and Andrew McLean was set for three o'clock that same afternoon. Barclay had been conducting pre-marriage seminars with Jill and Andrew for the past four months. It was going to be a big, splashy wedding…lots of invited guests on both sides of the families, a large wedding party with a flower girl and a ring bearer who both had little past association with the church. Potential problems loomed. The Friday night rehearsal event could be a time of chaos and frustration because of all the potential last-minute changes requested by the bride, and especially by the mother of the bride. Barclay was also committed to attending the wedding reception for Andrew and Jill set for seven thirty on Saturday evening. Faith would be going with him, even though she had not yet met Jill and Andrew, or any of the wedding attendants. How she dreaded these dinners. She only went to such occasions because she knew Barclay wanted her to be by his side at the dinner table. When a wedding takes place for people who have little or no association with the parish, it is always a huge problem for the person in charge of seating as to where to seat the priest. It helps to have her sit beside him. At least there is someone at the table who is not afraid to talk with him. Faith was a godsend in such circumstances.

Between the planning for the funeral and wedding and writing the homily for the coming Sunday, Barclay had finally managed to reach Harry Sting late on Thursday afternoon. Barclay explained how he and Faith had tickets to the symphony on Sunday evening and they were not prepared to miss the event. Harry was noticeably disappointed.

After Barclay was assured that Harry was not ill or in an emergency situation, they set the time for the dinner at the Sting's residence for six thirty. the following Sunday evening. Barclay remembered Faith's concern that Harry's wife was aware of the invitation. "Will this dinner a week from now be a concern for your spouse?" Barclay asked. Barclay had as of yet never heard Harry refer to his wife, not even her name.

"No, it will have to work. What I ask of her pretty well gets accepted. Sunday, a week from now will have to do."

That was a strange answer, Barclay thought to himself. Must be part of the puzzle for all the mystery of the coming get-together. Wait until Faith hears of that answer. "See you on Monday for the show, Harry. By the way, what is the topic for the day?" Barclay remembered the topic, but was hoping that Harry hadn't. Another topic, one more clearly defined, would be welcomed by Barclay.

But Harry hadn't forgotten. "The Marshmallow Church." Harry replied. "Should be fun. What do you think of that topic? Sorry, but there is another call coming in…got to go."

"The Marshmallow Church. What in the world was Harry driving at?" mused Barclay. "Guess I'll just have to wait and see what he has in his bonnet this time."

Chapter Twelve

NORMALLY, Barclay would schedule Friday night wedding rehearsals for six in the evening. With regular churchgoing people in the parish, one hour was always sufficient to set aside for the rehearsal event. Church people know the little subtleties of liturgical worship: how to dress properly when in the church; know by memory the words of the Creed, the Lord's Prayer, and the proper responses to say at the end of the readings; and know when to kneel and when to stand during worship. This is not the case when people who do not attend worship on a regular basis show up at the wedding rehearsal.

It would be no different this time when Jill and Andrew's friends and relatives arrive tonight. Not one of them, except for Jill and Andrew, were attending worship services at St. Bart's. So Barclay set the rehearsal time for four thirty. Besides, he and Faith were going to a play for seven thirty in the evening and he didn't want to be late for the performance. This would mean that he would have to decline the invitation to attend the wedding rehearsal dinner following the rehearsal event. In many ways, he was quite relieved to not have to show up. He knew that Jill and Andrew would certainly be disappointed, but the rest of the wedding party, he felt quite certain, would be quite relieved that he wouldn't be there and get in the way of their rowdy evening. In the eyes of the public, clergy are not quite human, so goes the general opinion of secular society. After all, what can a regular guy or gal say to a priest, except to ask him to say the grace at public functions?

The wedding rehearsal went more smoothly than Barclay expected. A couple of the bridesmaids, a groomsman, the flower girl, and ring bearer, Barclay was told, were to be fifteen minutes late, which meant that everyone had to put in time as they chatted with one another. Not being church folk, except for Andrew and Jill, Barclay could sense the nervousness of the group as they made small talk with each other. A couple of the groomsmen were wearing baseball caps. Two of the bridesmaids were carrying paper coffee cups, which presented a problem when they needed to dispose of the empty containers. One of the bridesmaids was surprised that there were no garbage cans in the nave. "Why not?" she asked. Barclay tactfully had to tell her that it wasn't the custom of parishioners to drink coffee in the church space set aside for worship. Garbage containers could be found in the parish hall. The baseball caps stayed on until the three late people finally arrived. At last they were ready to begin the rehearsal.

Barclay always began a wedding rehearsal with a prayer. This served a number of purposes. It immediately caused all excited conversation to cease, and males wearing a cap or hat were expected to remove it; if not, it provided Barclay with an opportunity to ask them to do so. Everyone began to prepare for the religious celebration the following day.

In the prayer Barclay asked God's blessing upon Jill and Andrew's upcoming marriage, and stressed the words "marriage covenant." He concluded the prayer with the request to ask everyone to say the Lord's Prayer together. Over the years, after conducting hundreds of weddings, Barclay could always tell how much of the church's teaching had been absorbed by those present for the rehearsal. If the Lord's Prayer was repeated in loud, clear sentences, Barclay knew that somewhere in the peoples' lives they had some exposure to the church. If Barclay ended up doing a monologue with no one else praying with him he knew that the sacred aspect of the wedding was missing in their minds.

After the Lord's Prayer one of the groomsmen hesitantly spoke up and asked Barclay what he meant by the words "marriage covenant." The teaching moment Barclay had hoped for had arrived.

"A covenant is an old fashioned word used over and over in the Old Testament," Barclay replied. "It was understood to be a mutual agreement that was sealed between God and a person or persons. It was a solemn promise that if the agreement was to be broken it would be the other party who did it. That means that if the agreement between God and a person was made, God would not break His word…it would have to be the human person who did so. And the person or persons promised that they would never break the agreement, but would wait for God to do so. Of course, God would never break His word, and so if the agreement was to be made null and void, it would have to be the person who broke it."

Barclay continued, "So, Jill and Andrew are making solemn vows tomorrow…marriage vows saying before God and all the congregation that if the marriage vows are to be broken the other person will end them. That means that Jill will have to wait for Andrew to break the vows and Andrew will have to wait for Jill to do so. In other words, each is promising the other that they will be faithful to each other forever."

"But," interrupted the exasperated groomsman, "what if they want to divorce sometime in the future? How can that happen if they each wait for the other to be the guilty party and not keep their marriage vows?"

"Ah," smiled Barclay, "now you've got it. If they are both stubborn and keep their end of the marriage vows then they have no choice but to work it out. After all, they will promise to do so tomorrow when they repeat these words before God, you, and me:

I Andrew/Jill take you Jill/Andrew,
to be my wife/husband,
to have and to hold
from this day forward;
for better, for worse,
in sickness and in health
to love and to cherish
for the rest of our lives,
according to God's holy law.
This is my solemn vow.

"Did you get that? 'My solemn vow?'" Barclay asked the future bride and groom.

Barclay could sense a change in the emotional tone of the little group preparing to go through the rehearsal routine. The group was obviously beginning to understand that a church wedding was serious business; lifelong promises were about to be made tomorrow, and all present were to be witnesses to those vows. It was time to begin the part of the rehearsal that would get the bridesmaids, groomsmen, flower girl, ring bearer, and parents of the bride and groom to their places for the formal part of the marriage liturgy. It was a fun time. After three attempts of getting the routine down pat, Barclay told them that it was going to be a wonderful day tomorrow.

"Well done." he said. "Now for a final few words to all. I know that tomorrow will be a time of celebration for all of you. It should be in every way. But remember this: if either the bride or groom should arrive for the wedding intoxicated, I by law, cannot perform the wedding. And this is very important as well: when I ask if there is any reason why these two cannot legally marry and someone stands up and says there is a reason, and the reason turns out to be a falsehood, by law I will call the police and that person will be arrested. But I know that no one here will be the one to do so. Tell your friends who might consider such a prank on the bride and groom not to dare try it!" With a final prayer the rehearsal ended.

It had gone well, much like hundreds of wedding rehearsals Barclay had conducted over the years. There could only be one possible hitch in the wedding tomorrow…the unpredictable antics of the precocious five-year-old ring bearer. If anyone were to do so, it would likely be himself to inject chaos into the liturgy.

CHAPTER THIRTEEN

SOME weeks seem to come and go much faster than others. The funeral service was well accepted by the grieving family and Andrew and Jill's wedding went off much more smoothly than Barclay had expected. Everyone arrived on time for the wedding, and the ceremony, to the organist's surprise and delight, started on time. Organists dread late beginnings. It means filling in with extra music until the liturgy can begin. Guests in the pews grow impatient and louder as the due time comes and passes. Small children need to take unexpected washroom breaks, and if more than one wedding is planned for the same day, clergy begin to fret that the earlier wedding will cut into the beginning time for the next one.

But not so that Saturday. Only one unexpected event took place. The young ring bearer, a delightful little fellow, smartly dressed in a sharp new suit, made it down the aisle just fine and was placed between the groom and the best man without fanfare. The flower girl stole the show, as flower girls always seem to do, and everyone in the wedding party seemed to remember their instructions, which had been practised at the rehearsal the night before. Well into the liturgy, Barclay noticed that the ring bearer was in trouble. He was shifting from foot to foot, a frown on his otherwise cherubic face. Barclay knew right away what the problem was…a washroom break was in order. The little fellow was holding the wedding rings, attached to the velvet pillow.

Would he be able to hold out until the best man was able to secure them from the cushion to give them to the priest when that part in the service, the blessing and exchange of rings, were to take place? The little fellow made it, to Barclay's delight and surprise. But a few minutes later in the liturgy Barclay looked down and the little fellow was gone. In the place where he had been standing was a wet circle of moisture on the red carpet beneath the wedding parties' feet. He had made it just so far…far enough so that the liturgy proceeded without interruption, but his disappearance was a major concern for his mother, who was one of the bridesmaids. She must have been racked by indecision…to not to leave or to leave to discover where her son had gone. She chose to stay in the line, but after the ceremony, her son at her side, she approached Barclay terribly upset and apologetic.

"Canon, can I pay for the cleaning of the carpet? What can I do to clean it?"

Barclay had to think quickly. "No, Susan, don't worry about it. I'm certain that St. Bartholomew's Parish can absorb it." One could literally see the worry in Susan's face dissipate as she got the pun. It was not the first time Barclay had experienced such a minor incident at a wedding, and it certainly wouldn't be the last.

Following the Saturday wedding, Barclay turned his attention to the upcoming two Sunday services. As usual, a large crowd was on hand for both. There was no doubt in his mind that his growing popularity on the Sting Show was the reason that church growth was occurring. But were people coming to worship for the right reasons, Barclay wondered? In the back of his mind he suspected that the curious were in the pews, not so much to worship God, but to get a first -hand glimpse of the man who was capable of putting Harry Sting in his place. This was beginning to be a concern for Barclay. He was enjoying himself nevertheless, and wasn't yet ready to cease being a foil to the notorious Harry Sting.

However, the upcoming Monday morning radio show with Harry, as far as Barclay was concerned, was going to be a waste of good airtime. Barclay was not sure what Harry had in mind when he had announced the topic "Marshmallow Church" to him over the phone. There was no way Barclay could prepare for what Harry had in mind for the show, but it turned out that Harry wanted to make the point that over the last few decades, the church, and Harry wouldn't concede which Christian denominations he had in mind, were slowly but surely softening theological standards of conduct for its members, and was therefore ever so slowly giving in to secular standards of the ever-changing modern culture. The point being, of course, that gradually the church was becoming a silent and irrelevant critic of morality. Who needs the church when the church appears to be in bed with modern mores, ethical standards, and flexible moral values? That was the point Harry seemingly wanted to make.

Harry was quite taken aback when early in the program Barclay confessed to Harry that he completely agreed with him. And thus Barclay totally threw Harry into a loss for further criticism of the church… and religion in general…by asking him, "Well, Harry, what do you expect the church to be in this modern age? What should the role of Christianity in today's times be?"

The program just didn't seem to be as adversarial as previous shows. How could it be, Barclay reflected, when they were both on the same page of the discussion?

Somehow, after the show ended, Barclay sensed that Harry had really wanted him to challenge society's 21st century "anything goes" values and thus rile up the listening audience to call in during the follow-up program after Barclay was no longer present. But maybe there was a deeper motive behind the topic. Perhaps Harry was longing for something that was now missing in his own life…perhaps a faith that he once grew up with, long since abandoned over the years.

Harry, Barclay concluded, was an enigma. There was something about him that Barclay was slowly beginning to respect and at the same time worry about…his on-air persona, the show business fellow who seemed to publically project such firmly held ideas and values, who, when off the air could demonstrate a totally different side of his personality. Barclay was soon to find answers to his troubling assessment of Harry.

The rest of the week passed without incident. Attendance was up at both Sunday services. People at the door following each service, were eager to press Barclay's hand as they left the church. "Keep up the good work, Doctor," they would say. "That Harry Sting deserves to be put in his place. He is a mean-spirited fellow and deserves to be cut down a peg or two!"

A few weeks ago, Barclay would probably have agreed with most of his adoring flock. But he now was troubled over his new-found understanding of who Harry Sting was. They were slowly becoming friends off air, but on air they continued to project the image of being enemies to the listening audience. Barclay knew that Harry was an entertainer and was just doing his job to keep ratings up for the station and generate revenue from the sponsors of the show. How long could he continue to keep up this charade of playing a game with Harry? Sure it was fun for both of the parties involved. But it was dishonest and Barclay knew it. Even so, it was good for St. Bart's parish.

After all, offerings were up with the ever-increasing numbers of new worshippers in the pews on Sunday mornings. And he was becoming somewhat of a star in Tangleville. "So what was wrong," Barclay reassured himself, "in using the show to promote Christianity in the town?" Surely, in this case, the end justified the means. So why was there that tiny burr irritating his conscience?

Sunday afternoon was a time of anxiety at the Steadmore's. Faith and Barclay had been instructed to arrive for dinner at the Stings late in the evening. That meant after sundown and so Faith and Barclay had plenty of time to get dressed and prepare for the event. Faith had purchased a simple arrangement of flowers to give to Harry's wife... neither of them yet knew her name. Barclay was so glad that Faith was coming with him. He was counting on her to help make conversation with the Stings that coming evening.

Faith had chosen to wear a rather conservative dress...one that Barclay felt didn't do justice to her figure...along with matching high-heeled shoes, and he, being instructed by Harry not to wear a clergy shirt and collar, decided to dress in a pair of Dockers jeans and a striped open-necked shirt and a navy sports jacket. If the neighbors were watching, no one would suspect that the Stings' guests were really a cleric and his spouse. Certainly not in the darkness of the evening. Harry had said that the porch light would not be turned on when they were to arrive.

In a heady sort of way, Faith and Barclay were excited about their visit to the Stings. It certainly looked as if the evening could generate intrigue for both of them. "Care to speculate what is going to happen Bark?" Faith queried as Barclay opened the door of the Jeep Liberty, allowing her to slip into the front passenger seat.

"Haven't got a clue, Faith. Let's just go for it."

"I do." said Faith, "but I'm not going to spoil your evening in advance." There she was again, her old self with that intuitive side of her nature tuned into future happenings.

Barclay, as usual, was completely in the dark. "Don't tell me," Barclay agreed. "I want to respond to tonight's events just as they unfold, without pre-conceived guesses as to what could happen." This was one night that Barclay was really looking forward to.

CHAPTER FOURTEEN

FAITH and Barclay arrived at Harry's residence at precisely seven thirty. Harry had informed Barclay not to arrive during daylight hours, and during this time of the year it was already nightfall. The streetlights on Upper Manhattan Crescent were already on, and true to Harry's warning, the porch light was not burning. It was bright enough from the city street lights to make out that Harry's residence was a magnificent one...two stories, a triple-car garage and a wide driveway leading up to the entrance. One door of the garage was open and Barclay could make out that a shiny red 1972 Jaguar XKE convertible was parked inside.

"Faith," Barclay whispered to her as they walked arm in arm up to the front door: "Did you see that sports car? At least Harry has great taste in cars. I didn't know that he is a car guy."

"Never noticed," replied Faith. "Maybe the car belongs to his wife. What did you say her name is?"

"Harry has never told me a single thing about her," Barclay replied. "Your guess is as good as mine."

Barclay pressed the doorbell and it seemed to take an unexpectedly long time for the door to finally open. Faith and Barclay looked at each other in the semi-darkness, smiling, as if to say, "Do you suppose we came too early?" The door opened and there stood Harry, dressed in a neatly pressed pair of gray trousers, a very fashionable silk dress shirt, topped off with a pair of black loafers that shone in the light of the entranceway.

"Welcome, Barclay. Come in," he said, as he warmly grasped Barclay's hand and then turned toward Faith. "I'm so happy to finally meet you, Faith!" As surprised as Barclay was that Harry remembered Faith's name, she wasn't. She had already extended her hand to him as he squeezed it in a warm and inviting manner.

Faith greeted Harry with that becoming smile of hers that always immediately endeared her to strangers. "Harry, I've heard so much about you," she replied. "It's wonderful to finally meet you face to face."

Harry took Barclay's sports jacket, hung it in the hall closet, and led them into the living room. A fire was burning in the fireplace, and both Barclay and Faith quickly recognized that it was an opulent room, tastefully furnished with expensive furniture. Harry and his wife obviously were doing well with radio station AM KNOW.

And then a petite, stunning brunette entered the room. Barclay immediately stood up, and Harry was quick to introduce his wife to his guests. "Faith, Barclay, this is Anastasia…but everyone calls her Annie."

Annie greeted Faith with a kiss on her left and right cheeks and grasped Barclay's right hand in both of hers. "Welcome! We are so glad that you could come."

It was a most unexpected first meeting with Annie. What an exceptional hostess she turned out to be! Barclay wondered how in the world two people could be so different: the on-air, belligerent Harry…

his public side for consumption by his listening radio audience…and the warm, gracious, refined Annie. It didn't seem to add up, Barclay thought to himself. Annie and Faith were already engaged in congenial conversation over in front of the fireplace, and Harry had returned after taking orders for something to drink. Annie had placed the flowers Faith had presented to her in a beautiful vase and placed them on a stand next to the fireplace.

The meal was a wonderful relaxing time together. Harry asked Barclay to bless the food before they began to eat and at the close of the prayer Barclay noticed that Annie crossed herself. Harry didn't, but Barclay really didn't expect he would, given his on-air tirades about his disdain for faith and religion.

The roast beef dinner was absolutely delicious. Barclay's portion of meat was done exactly medium-rare, as he hoped it would be, and Faith's well done, as she preferred it. The meal ended with blueberry pie topped with french vanilla ice cream, coffee, and a couple of small after-dinner mints.

"Barclay, let's retire to my study downstairs," Harry suggested to Barclay. "Annie is an artist and I have some of her work there that I want you to see. Meanwhile, she and Faith can get together on their own for a while. Follow me."

"Here it comes…he wants some private time with me," thought Barclay as Annie and Faith moved together into the den. Downstairs in Harry's study would surely be out of earshot to the women upstairs.

Harry's study was large, with two walls covered with books. Perhaps, if he could somehow do so, he would quickly browse the titles filling the shelves. It would give him some information about Harry's reading habits and what his real interests in life are. But what overwhelmed him was the array of watercolor and oil paintings tastefully hanging on the other two walls. "These are some of Annie's work," Harry pointed out to Barclay. "They are the ones she didn't feel are up to her standards for public sale." Barclay was simply speechless. Harry had never mentioned that his spouse was an accomplished artist. Furthermore, her name as he had just learned, 'Anastasia' did not appear on the lower right side of each piece of work. Rather, there was the name A.F. Antonov, the famous artist that everyone who was familiar with contemporary painting would instantly recognize. Barclay had observed some of her work hanging in the art gallery in downtown Tangleville.

"Harry, what is the name A.F. Antonov about?"

"Oh, that is her maiden name. She signs that way on all her work," Harry responded. "She was a painter long before we were married and always kept that signature." This was turning out to be an evening far beyond Barclay's expectations.

Harry and Barclay sat down facing each other in the two comfortable leather chairs a few feet in front of Harry's large mahogany desk. "Barclay, there is something I want to talk about tonight," Harry blurted out. "Can we talk in complete confidence? As a priest, I'm sure that you know what I'm asking." Barclay, now assuming the role of the confessor, simply nodded in the affirmative, and waited for Harry to continue.

There was a long silence as Harry's eyes seemed to be glued to the floor in front of him. Then he began to speak. "Barclay, I'm a hypocrite," he finally blurted in a voice that was soft and measured. Barclay didn't reply, but simply waited for Harry to continue. Another long silent period indicated to Barclay how difficult this conversation was going to be for his host this evening. This was a far different side of Harry from that of his persona on The Harry Sting Show.

"Harry, the word 'hypocrite' is a loaded word…a word that wears two hats, if I may put it that way…a Biblical meaning and the common secular one. What do you mean by the statement that you first made to me?"

Another long silence indicated that Harry was searching for words. Barclay waited for Harry's answer. "Both, Barclay. Both," he finally stammered in a faltering voice.

"Let's take it one at a time, Harry. Which meaning do you want to discuss first?"

"I want to start with my radio show. I'm at the point where I dread going into work every day. The management is delighted with the ratings. I'm making a good salary. No matter where I go people recognize me. When they do, I'm, either hailed as a hero or as a heretic. That doesn't bother me as much as perhaps it should. But deep down inside I've come to the point where I can't live with myself. I think that you already know this, but on the show I'm nothing more than an actor behind the microphone. It's all a charade…an act. I'm not being authentic and I can't live with it much longer. I simply don't know what to do."

Barclay knew that Harry was finally dealing with long-seated issues in his life, but Harry wasn't there yet. It would take more time and more probing to finally get to the root of the matter. Barclay was, if anything, a listener…time was going to be needed if Harry was going to resolve his concerns.

"Harry, what if the management offered you a substantial increase in salary? Would that be enough to keep you in the show?" Barclay deliberately used the word "show" to convey to Harry that he understood what Harry meant by the choice of his words: an act or a charade. He was quite sure that Harry would catch on to the fact that as a priest he understood what was being said in his admission of stress and concern.

"Barclay, they could double my salary and that wouldn't make an iota of difference in how I feel. Besides, Annie and I don't need the money. She makes far more than I do. Her paintings sell for thousands and thousands of dollars. I could quit work today and never miss my present salary. Money is not a factor in our lives."

"Great," responded Barclay as he leaned a little forward in his comfortable leather chair. "We have now just established that monetary matters are not going to solve your problem. I suspect that there are other factors in your life that are highly influencing this need for our conversation. Am I right?"

There was another long silence and finally Harry looked at Barclay straight in the face and said, "I think that I'm going to have to deal with some spiritual issues in my life. I don't know how to do this and where to begin."

"Harry, there is no better place to begin than at the beginning of your life. Let's go there. Let's put on your spiritual hat. Do you have a spiritual hat?"

Barclay knew that Harry would instantly recognize the kind of role-play that both had used on the many radio shows they had done together…the times when Barclay would respond to Harry's aggressive questioning by saying, "Do you want me to wear my spiritual hat or my secular hat to answer your question?"

There was an ever-so-slight smile that crossed Harry's face. He knew exactly what Barclay was challenging him to discuss. "Barclay," Harry began, "I grew up in a home where religion was never discussed. My parents were agnostics…perhaps even closer to being atheists. The notion of a God was considered to be folly, not worthy of concern for intelligent people. I grew up thinking that I was a moral person, kind, thoughtful, tolerant...even generous, and concerned for my fellow beings. Not because I believed that there is a God to recommend those virtues to me, but because they were the right things to do. In other words, 'to do unto others what you would have them do unto you.'"

"Go on, Harry," Barclay motioned. "I'm listening."

"But then I married Annie. Annie's upbringing was a polar oppo-site one to mine. She was baptized and confirmed in the Russian Orthodox faith and follows its teachings even to this day. She goes to church every Sunday, and even on weekly high days. She is a devout Christian and is gentle and absolutely comfortable in her faith. She's kind, never critical, generous to a fault, and so considerate of others. A woman of faith! And Barclay, I know that she has been praying for me for some twenty-four years now following our marriage. She loves me without ever criticizing me. She accepts me for who I am, but here is the rub...she knows that I am not a Christian, a believer in Christ, and am far from practicing her Christian principles. She, I know, absolutely believes that God will answer her prayers and that someday I will be a believer and will be baptized and confirmed. And Barclay, somehow I am now having to face the fact that I don't know why, or even understand, that I'm having a spiritual and moral crisis in my life. What is going on Barclay? I'm at my wits end."

"Maybe you will have to finally admit that God exists, Harry. Are you there yet?"

"I don't know, Barclay. But I want to tell you that being with you these past weeks on the radio show...I mean, that has not helped my situation. You and Annie are just too much alike. I know that you are an Anglican, not of Annie's denomination, but you are both so comfortable in your spiritual skins. You've both got something that I don't have and I'm finally at the point in my life that I envy you both. Tell me what is happening in my life."

"I think that you already know, Harry. I can explain it by telling you that the Holy Spirit is speaking to you, but I'm not sure that's what you want to hear. What do you think that you are being led to do at this point in your faith journey?"

"Barclay, I've got in my mind two problems. I don't think that I can continue my role as it now exists with The Harry Sting Show, and…I'm ready to admit it…that I think that I've got to investigate further into this thing called Christianity."

"Harry, you really don't have two problems, you only have one. One will solve the other, if you choose to wear the right hat. Do you know what I'm talking about?"

"I think that I do, Barclay. I think that you are saying that my lack of Christian conviction and faith is the root of the problem, and if that was settled my role as a host on the show would also be defined. Right?"

"You've got it, Harry! So where do you think you've got to go from here?"

"That's where I need your help, Barclay. How do I go about my life? Who I am, or perhaps, better put, who I need to become?"

"Harry, if you first deal with your lack of a Christian commitment, the rest of your life choices will fall into place. Why don't you begin to attend Christian services with Annie? I'm sure that she will be overjoyed to have you as her pew partner. Why don't you talk to her priest? I'm sure that they have classes for conversion to the faith."

"I can't do that Barclay. All their services, their liturgies, are in Russian. I don't speak a word of Russian."

"Okay! Here is a second alternative. We at St. Bartholomew's hold annual classes for those who wish to be baptized and later confirmed. How would you feel about joining the class? It begins in about three weeks, is always held on a Wednesday evening, and goes for six weeks in duration. I lead it and you and I can meet outside the classes anytime you need to discuss further concerns you may have. How does that sound?"

"But what about my radio show? I've just admitted how much I resent going into work each morning. I just admitted that a while ago that in the show I'm a hypocrite. What should I do about that?"

"Harry, you've got the most loyal listeners of all AM KNOW's programs in Tangleville. Your boss loves you. Why don't you in the weeks ahead discuss with management how you would like to remake the show into one that asks questions… really deep, important questions in life, such as the meaning of life, the value of faith in peoples' lives, what real happiness is, how to deal with failure and disappointments. Invite guests on the show, experts in the community, people who have experienced in real time each of these topics and discuss the no end of concerns that people out there in the audience are likely experiencing. Experts as well as ordinary people…survivors, victims, people who have overcome adverse conditions. You will have more people wanting to get on your show than you can possibly admit. Slowly transform your now confrontational show into one that investigates overcoming peoples' personal problems, and in so doing, become a loved and admired host who really cares about people and their concerns. People will eventually begin to wonder what has happened to the once caustic, religion-hating Harry Sting. And it won't take long for them to begin to inquire about your personal faith stance. Doors will open and you can ever so slowly begin to address your own faith stance with people who may wish to emulate your journey in Christ.

But one step at a time, Harry. First talk it over with Annie. Be sure that she is on side…I'm betting that she will be right there with you all the way. It may be one of the most risky chances you will ever take at AM KNOW. But if God is behind all this, you can't fail, no matter what may take place. You told me money is not a factor in your marriage. What have you got to lose if they say no and fire you? In the end you will find meaning and happiness in your life and marriage and be able to hold your head high in knowing who you really are. Stop trying to wear two hats and instead wear the one that really fits your real inner self."

"Barclay, I'm going to think about it. I'm going to have a long talk with Annie. Can I get back to you with what we come up with?"

Barclay nodded in the affirmative. He mentally noted that Harry had used the word "think" instead of the verb that most people use in such a point in one's life, the word "pray." But Harry was not a man of prayer, and when Barclay finally grasped Harry's hand he looked him straight in the eye and said, "I'll pray for you in my daily devotions." A tear, a single tear, rolled down from each of Harry's eyes and he quickly turned his back to Barclay to feign blowing his nose.

"I've got a problem with allergies, Barclay. Excuse me for a moment." Barclay wisely said nothing, but inwardly smiled to himself.

It was one of the most touching moments in both Harry's and Barclay's lives. They hugged each other, and Harry, a big man, forcefully steered Barclay to the stairs leading to the den on the first floor. Faith and Annie were sitting close to one another, deeply engaged in conversation. It was obvious to both Harry and Barclay that they were becoming friends.

"Faith, we've stayed far too late with these good folks, it seems. Harry has a show tomorrow and we should be saying our goodbyes. We can get together soon. What do you say?"

Faith could read Barclay like a book after so many years of marriage. "I know it's late and Annie and I have so many things to discuss. Let's get together, Annie, in the very near future," she said as she and Annie kissed each other on the cheeks. There were warm words of goodbye and thank-yous from both sides. As Barclay and Faith exited the front entrance, the garage door was still open and the Jaguar XKE was clearly visible from the walkway.

"Harry, I would really like you to someday take me for a ride in your Jag. How about it?" Barclay asked.

"Oh, the Jag is Annie's, Barclay. She seldom lets me behind the wheel. But I'm sure she would be happy to do so herself. She is the 'car guy' in the house." Faith smiled at Barclay. Once again another of her predictions had come true.

Chapter Fifteen

BECAUSE of an eleven o'clock funeral service at St. Bartholomew's Church, Barclay was unable to do the show with Harry at AM KNOW on the Monday following his and Faith's visit to the Sting residence. Barclay did not hear from Harry during the following week. Somehow Barclay did not expect to. Harry had said that he wanted to think about his future as a radio show host. Barclay suspected that there was a great deal more going on in Harry's life than a change of venue at AM KNOW, if his show was to indeed continue. Now Barclay understood that Harry was experiencing a spiritual crisis. Barclay remembered that as they concluded their time together in Harry's den, Harry didn't say that he would pray about a new direction in his life, but rather that he would think about it. Barclay assumed that that was precisely what was happening. If only Harry would confide in Annie that he was seeking to alter his life. Annie was as unshakeable in her Christian faith as Harry was lost in his search for new beginnings.

On Saturday morning, the rectory telephone rang. Faith answered and after a few minutes of cordial conversation she passed the cordless phone to Barclay and said, "It's for you!"

"Barclay speaking," he replied.

"Good morning, Doctor, it's Harry."

"Good morning, Harry. It's good to hear from you. How are things going?"

"Okay, I think. I've been doing a lot of thinking during the past few days since we last talked. Are you free Monday morning to do your weekly show with me?" I want to try something a little different on the broadcast. I want to try to make it an educational, not a confrontational format...not like what we have been doing in the past. Can you make it? I know that it is short notice, but I'm dying to try something new."

"Harry, you know that I begged off last Monday, but it sounds intriguing. What do you want to attempt to explore on the air? After all, I want to show up wearing the right hat, if you know what I mean."

"I agree. I want to tackle the topics of atheism, agnosticism, and faith in a Supreme Being."

"Where are you going with this Harry? Be a little more specific before I say yes or no."

"Barclay, I want to have you explain to my audience what each of those terms really means. I don't think people out there really understand the consequences of claiming to be one or the other. Is it reasonable to claim to be such a person? To tell you the truth, I have never thought about it myself, up until now. I'm not going to take sides on the show. I'm simply planning to confront the audience out there to begin thinking about such matters. The second half hour should take care of itself."

Barclay was quick to catch on to what Harry was saying between the lines. It really wasn't a matter of educating the listening public. It was an admission of his own personal interest at stake, and perhaps, an attempt to modify the format of his show. "Good for you Harry." thought Barclay. "God works in mysterious ways."

"Harry, I think that I can be there. I believe that you're on the right track after our conversation last week. I'll show up a half hour before the show so that we can agree to be on the same page for the broadcast. By the way, how is Annie? Say 'hello' to her for us."

"She's fine…out somewhere with her Jag. It is a beautiful day so she has the top down. I'll give her your greetings. Thanks Barclay. See you Monday morning."

Barclay could hardly wait for Monday to arrive. He was anxious to meet with Harry early before the show to nail down what was going to be discussed on the broadcast. Barclay spent considerable time after Harry's call to do research on the topics of atheism and agnosticism. They were topics that as a priest he had spent little time thinking about or studying in his years of seminary training. There surely would be people calling into the show in the second half of Harry's program who will passionately be defending their claims of not believing in a supreme being. Perhaps Harry was onto something if he really was sincere in altering the format of his usual antagonist approach to religious values and faith in the lives of people and society.

Barclay pulled into the parking lot at AM KNOW forty-five minutes early for the broadcast. The receptionist at the front desk welcomed him with a warm smile and hurriedly ushered him toward Harry's office. "The boss is waiting for you," she said. "He seems to be a bit anxious this morning. I hope that he's okay."

Harry's office door was open. Harry jumped to his feet, grasped Barclay's hand, and steered him to one of the two big leather chairs that were positioned before his own office desk. Harry, to Barclay's surprise, did not return to sit in his big chair parked behind his desk, but instead sat down beside Barclay, leaning forward as he spoke: "I'm glad you're here, Doctor. I really want this morning to begin something new for my show. And I think you are the only one I know who can help me do it."

Barclay and Harry spent the next thirty minutes agreeing how the first one-half hour of the show would go. They agreed that Harry would say how he wanted to begin something totally different in his hosting of a new educational program for the town of Tangleville. In the future he would be inviting professional experts as guests to discuss areas of living so that his listeners could then become more informed in making important choices that would enrich their lives. It would be the same one-hour time frame as before. The guest would be interviewed in the first half-hour and the listening audience could call in to challenge or agree with what they had heard during the first segment of The Harry Sting Show in the second half-hour. Barclay really liked what he was hearing. Together they walked into the broadcasting booth and took their places behind their microphones, a good five minutes before the ten o'clock deadline for the show to begin.

Barclay could sense that Harry was a little more nervous than usual as they waited for the ON AIR light to flash. But somehow Barclay knew that it would be a great show...a new beginning for Harry. He had been praying for Harry for some time now...that God would intervene in Harry's life so that he would become an ambassador for the Christian faith. This morning was to be an answer to his prayers.

The ON AIR sign flashed and Harry's professional voice took over the show.

> *"Good morning, thinking people of Tangleville. It's Monday morning and I know that you will sense that something new and exciting is taking place on this and*

future shows. A new criteria for choosing guests for the first-half hour is now in place. In the future, invited guests will be professionals who will bring you, the listening audience, authoritative facts and information about current, controversial issues in society. Instead of me confronting and challenging what the guests will be presenting, I will instead act as the facilitator and moderator… the one who helps by asking questions of our guests to clarify what they are presenting to us. The big difference in this and future shows is that you, in the second-half, will become the challenging critics of what our guests will have to present to this great town of Tangleville. So you, then, become the sharp-minded adjudicators who will sift the chaff from the wheat, so to speak. Now, what does that really mean? It means that you, the listening audience, people who were previously merely entertained by our first-half-hour format, will be challenged to become far more involved in a thoughtful, rational way, sharing your views in the phone-in segment of the show. I do not merely want your opinion about what you feel and think, but why you think and feel that way. Back up your calls with logical, well thought out argumentation. I, as the host, will be challenging you to defend your positions. Do you think you are up to it? We shall see.

Now, who better to kick off this new format of my show than today's well-known guest, The Reverend Canon Doctor Barclay Steadmore, rector of St. Bartholomew's Anglican Parish here in Tangleville? Today's topic…what is the rationale for atheism, agnosticism, and believers in

a divine creator in today's secular society? "Good morning
and welcome, Doctor Steadmore."

"Good morning, Harry. Great to be here. I'm excited about your new plans. Thank you for inviting me as your first guest to initiate your revised show."

"So where and how do we begin today, Canon? You are a man of faith, as everyone who listens to this show for the past broadcasts knows. But there are many out there in the listening audience today who call themselves atheists, or even agnostics. How do we in our secular age explain such a wide variance in peoples' attempts to wrestle with the belief in the concept of a divine creator? Are those who don't, or won't agree with you simply wrong? What do you, a theologian, have to say to such people?

"Harry, you just used the word 'faith'…you said that I am a man of faith. Let's examine what faith means when we talk about the notion of a divine creator…a creator God."

"Okay, explain what you mean then by 'belief.'"

"When it comes to the existence of God, Harry, there is no absolute proof, so to speak, that such a Being exists. We cannot prove that God exists, and we cannot prove that He doesn't exist. So when it comes to the acceptance, or rejection of the existence of God, we are then theists and atheists on common ground. We both then are stating our positions on the basis of belief, not fact. We are, of course, on opposite sides of the concept, but we are in the same category for stating our cases…belief. So, when an atheist talks about disbelief in God, it's really an act of faith…the belief that no God exists. Similarly, the believer in a divine creator also expresses one's position, not on fact, not by proof, but as a statement of belief."

"So what does it then leave us with, Barclay? That whoever, or whichever side can produce the best argument wins?"

"That's an interesting way of putting it, Harry. But the fact is, neither God's existence nor His non-existence depends one iota on which human side wins the argument. Either God is, or He isn't. We have absolutely no part in the matter. What matters is...and let's be absolutely honest here...the consequences of whether He exists or not. Do you see where I'm going, Harry?"

"Go on Barclay. So far, so good. I'm with you!"

"You see Harry, both atheists and theists, or believers, have another thing in common besides a faith position. We are both gamblers!"

"Wait a minute Barclay! Gamblers? I've never expected you to call yourself a gambler. Now you've lost me!"

"Well, since we can't prove God exists, we're both betting our lives on the matter, but both positions are diametrically opposed to each other and so one side has to be wrong and one side has to be right. However, the consequences of winning or losing are catastrophic."

"How so?"

"Suppose for a minute that the atheist gambles on the premise that God does not exist. In a certain sense, he or she is a winner in that if God does not exist there is no possibility of divine judgment following one's earthly passing. Therefore, no heaven and no hell. No casting into 'outer darkness' as we theologians like to say. The only judgment of the deceased is the legacy one leaves behind in the world. For example, take Hitler. His judgment would be for human history, not one that a just God will deal with. So, if no God exists then the atheist is a winner at least in the sense that one does not have to face the possibility of eternal damnation.

"But...and here is the risk such a gambler takes...if God does exist, and one has deliberately denied his existence, then according to the Christian faith, that individual will spend eternity in hell. I don't know of any easier or kinder way to put it!"

"But you said that a believer in a divine creator is also a gambler. How so?"

"Harry, if one gambles that God exists, then one has to face the demands one understands that God places on human conduct while in this world. So, then, a trade-off must begin in one's life. In order to conform to the perceived standards God lays down for His followers, certain restrictions are thus self-imposed on one's earthy life. The Ten Commandments, for example, do not become the 'ten suggestions.' Our Lord's commandment to love the Lord our God with all our heart, and with all our soul, and with all our mind, and with all our strength, and to love our neighbors as ourselves then takes priority over personal behavior and conduct in this earthly life. One then gambles on the placing of a higher priority on winning a heavenly reward over license and personal freedom in their life."

"So Canon, a believer loses out in this earthly world if one puts limits and restrictions on one's earthly lifestyle in order to have the hope of eternal salvation? I think that is what you are saying...that a reward for eternity trumps a limited reward of unrestricted choices during one's earthly existence."

"That's what you might conclude, Harry. But, you see, a believer wins in spite of whether God exists or not. If no God exists, then of course, no divine judgment. No heavenly reward either. You might conclude that a believer is a loser in this respect. But not so, because even if no God and no heavenly reward exist, one's earthly life as a believer is immensely enriched in spite of placing self-restrictions on one's lifestyle. For those self-restrictions have so many benefits to the self and to society. Peace of mind, lack of guilt, guaranteed friends and acceptance of a like-minded community, the church, no constant need to defend one's position as atheists always seem to feel is necessary in defending their arguments for their faith stance, a lifestyle that in many cases is one of moderation and self -control which in the end has definite long-term health advantages. There are obligatory, self-imposed restrictions on how one spends one's finances…a built-in basis to support charities and the poor and the disposed…in other words, an obligation not merely left up to chance, but an understanding of how the Holy Scriptures place requirements on a believer's life. Believers thus have a built-in sense of purpose. A believer does not abide by the old adage of 'live it up for today, because tomorrow you die.' All of this gives believers a sense of well-being, hope for the future, and a reason for one's existence. Life is not understood as a matter of sheer chance, an accident of a non-planned universe. A believer is a winner if God exists or He doesn't exist. Living the Christian life is a win-win effort."

"Canon, why can't an atheist enjoy all the same lifetime pleasures and experiences that you just said are enjoyed by believers?"

"Because, Harry, atheists always seem to be feeling the need to defend their belief system of a universe that they claim came into being by sheer chance, thus placing themselves in the state of having no divine purpose, no rationale for being other than ceasing to be at some time in the future. How can such a lack of purpose and meaninglessness generate happiness and well-being? The only real choice then is to cram in as much experiential stimuli as one can generate in order to divert one's attention away from the fatalistic end of claimed non-existence following death. For atheists life becomes a cosmic joke."

"That's heavy, Canon! I wonder what my callers during the second portion of this show will have to say. But I can certainly understand how what you just told us may be true. Life without purpose has got to be meaningless."

"Harry, the Holy Scriptures sum it up, claiming a believer's life is one of hope, love, peace, joy, contentment, and purpose...in this world and the next."

"But Canon, you haven't yet touched on the existence of agnostics. Who are they? How do they differ from atheists and believers?"

"Agnosticism is the view that the true value of certain claims, especially claims about the existence of a deity, are unknown or unknowable."

"Isn't there some truth in their claims?"

"Yes, indeed. But agnosticism goes beyond dealing only with the question of whether God exists or not...it claims that all attempts to know the reality of God are futile. Agnosticism reaches as well into scientific and philosophical areas of human conduct. Agnosticism is a term of modern philosophy that states that there are limitations of human knowledge, the existence of 'absolute reality' is usually affirmed, while at the same time, its knowableness is denied. People like Herbert Spencer, that great philosopher, biologist, anthropologist, sociologist, and literal political theorist of the Victorian Age and Henry Longueville Mansel, the Anglican theologian in the 1800s made this affirmation the central basis of their philosophical systems.

"So, in short, true agnostics deny that it is possible for human beings on their own to acquire knowledge of a supreme being. We don't need, for the sake of time, to go into a much deeper understanding here this morning than to apply its concept to religion alone. Let's leave science and philosophy in agnosticism for a future discussion.

"However, just for the fun of it, let me add that Ancesilaus, that ancient Greek philosopher a couple of centuries before the time of Christ, stated that 'total or complete agnosticism is self-refuting.' He used the famous formula "I know nothing" and said it can't be questioned. So he claimed that it is impossible to construct theoretically a self-consistent scheme of total doubt, and unbelief. Neat, wouldn't you say?"

"Don't go there, Steadmore! Stick to the topic of religion only."

"So you see, Harry, theists and agnostics differ when it comes to a belief in the existence of God as theists state that the question of knowing God is not the same as the question of defining Him. The two do not stand or fail together. For theists argue that revelation offers believers historical truth of the existence of God. Faith begins where science and philosophy end. No agnostic would entertain truth through revelation of God to humankind. The agnostic denial of the ability of human reason to know God through His means of revealing Himself to humanity is directly opposed to orthodox Christians. Does this help?"

"Okay! Okay! So in summary, what do you have to say about agnostics? You came down on atheists as spiritual losers in both this world and possibly the next. Are you going to be kinder in your treatment of agnostics?"

"Harry, I have to admit that Christians can tolerate true agnostics in a better light than atheists, for there is always the possibility with genuine agnostics that if they meet and associate with true Christians, they could even be persuaded to become one. Not so with atheists, I'm afraid. I believe that agnostics are intellectually honest and do not carry a bias for or against the notion of a divine being. I like that!"

"Barclay, we only have about two minutes left in this broadcast segment. What do you want to say in a closing statement before the listening audience in the next half-hour takes over?"

"Well, let me tell you a story: A philosopher shared a seat with a small boy on a shuttle train. The boy was holding a Sunday school book.

"Do you go to Sunday school, my boy?" asked the professor in a friendly way.

"Yes, sir."

"Tell me, my boy," continued the learned man, thinking that he would have some fun with the young lad. "Tell me where God is and I'll give you an apple."

The boy replied, "I will give you a whole barrel of apples if you tell me where He is not."

Harry reached over and shook Barclay's hand. "I guess it is true what Voltaire said: 'If God did not exist, it would be necessary to invent Him.'"

As the ON AIR sign went off Barclay's mind was in high gear. "Now what in the world would cause Harry to say that?"

Chapter Sixteen

ON his way back to St. Bartholomew's, Barclay tuned into radio station AM KNOW to listen to the second half-hour of Harry's program, the section where the listening audience was to have its opportunity to challenge what he had presented in the first section.

The lines were full, according to Harry. Obviously, the first half-hour had stirred up great interest in Harry's listeners. That is exactly what Harry had told him he wanted to see happen. Now it was up to Harry to take them on, one caller at a time. What was going to be interesting was to see how Harry could do that. Would there be any indication as to which side of Barclay's presentation that Harry would appear to be favoring? Could the listening audience detect a hint of bias that Harry was moving toward his own faith discovery?

It only took a few minutes for Barclay to reach St. Bart's. There was no time to listen to the rest of the second half-hour. Piles of work that needed his attention were waiting on his desk. As he passed Hannah, who was busy at her desk, he could not help but overhear that she was tuned into The Harry Sting Show on the office radio.

"Good morning, Hannah. Hold my calls for an hour or so if you can...all those that you deem can wait for me to call back. Of course, if Bishop Strictman calls, put him through right away. We all know that he doesn't like to be put on hold. If Bill Stern calls, he can wait." Hannah smiled that knowing smile of hers.

"The usual procedures, right?"

"You're good, Hannah! I don't know what St. Bartholomew's would do without you. And, oh yes, keep your ear tuned to the tone of the call-in folks on Harry's show. You can tell me how it's going for Harry. I'll pour myself a cup of tea on my way into my office."

Barclay shut his office door and wrote his monthly report to Bishop Strictman, outlining his evaluation of how his relationship with Harry Sting on the show was going. He did not mention their visit to the Sting residence. There would be plenty of time later on to talk to his Bishop about the event. Nor did he tell Bishop Strictman about his feelings that Harry was undergoing a spiritual awakening. After all, he could have misjudged Harry's informal confession during that time they spent downstairs in Harry's study. At this juncture of the evolution of Harry Sting, time would tell the story better than his guessing would.

The weekly outline of next week's bulletin had been prepared by Hannah. He read the lessons for the following Sunday and spent about half an hour attempting to find a text from one of them for his Sunday homily. Nothing was jumping out of the readings so far, which caused him to do further research in the Biblical commentaries in his library. "Let it sit for a while," he thought to himself. "It will come. It always does!"

Exactly one-and-a-half hours after he had entered his office…the time seemed to have flown by…his office intercom buzzed. It was Hannah. "Doctor, Harry is on the line. Are you free to talk with him?"

"Good morning Harry. You sound chipper at this time of the day. What's up?"

"Barclay, it was the best second half I've had in years! The lines were completely jammed from the minute you and I finished the first-half section. I can't believe it."

"What do you think that means, Harry?"

"It means that I'm onto something in trying out a new format for the show. Two callers actually thanked me for being civil with you, my guest. Three others accused me of becoming a convert to the church."

"Well, how did you respond to those three? I'd be curious to know what you said."

"I simply repeated what I said to you as we signed off, remember? The Voltaire quote: "If God did not exist, it would be necessary to invent Him.""

"Well put, Harry, but what's really important is whether you mean what you said, or was it merely another clever show business tactic to counter your listeners' accusations?"

"Barclay, can we get together again? Soon?

"Of course, Harry, but I'm not prepared to meet you again incognito, so to speak. You know, coming to your home after dark without my clerical collar on. If you want to come to my office here at St. Bart's it's a deal!"

To Barclay's complete surprise, Harry responded, "When can we do it?"

"Tomorrow morning at eleven thirty. The weather for tomorrow is supposed to be clear and sunny. You will possibly be spotted coming to the parish. Still want to do it?"

"I'll be there! What do you take in your coffee?"

"Double cream, Harry! See you tomorrow."

Barclay, needless to say, was lost for words. He walked out of his office and could hardly wait to talk to Hannah. "How did that second half-hour go Hannah?"

"Doctor, I've never listened to anything like it. The audience was completely divided in its responses. About two-thirds of them gave you a thumbs up on what you said in the first segment, and the rest were absolutely defiant, disagreeing with everything you said... especially since you used the word 'gambler.' Harry was having the time of his life!"

"Hannah, did Harry seem to lean toward either side of their arguments? Did he give one side or the other what might be deemed as his approval?"

"He was careful...extremely careful in that regard. Maybe I'm reading more than I should into the situation, but when he quoted, you know, the words of Voltaire, he seemed to be taking great delight in putting down the atheists. You would almost think that he believed in what he was saying."

"Thank you, Hannah. Time will tell, I suppose. What have you booked on my agenda for this afternoon?"

That afternoon Barclay made three home communion visits to those who were shut-ins at nursing homes, as well as two hospital visits. He managed to arrive home for dinner at five thirty, exhausted but very satisfied with the day's events.

Faith was busy in the kitchen and from the moment that he entered the door, it was obvious from the aroma that a roast beef dinner awaited him. She knew from their many years of marriage that he enjoyed nothing better than a rare cut of roast beef, smothered in dark gravy. Now if only he could detect the smell of a fresh-baked blue-berry pie!

Faith and Barclay sat down for dinner in their comfortable, but quite ordinary, practically decorated dining room. They had not replaced much of the furniture that was still showing the wear and tear of raising a family of two active children now all grown up, married, and living out of town. "Why bother," Barclay had said, "when there is always the hope of having grandchildren around the house? We both know how rambunctious they can be." Faith wasn't convinced, however.

After coffee Faith took over the conversation. "Barclay, while you were at work today Annie and I got together. She picked me up in her Jag XKE, the top down, and we went shopping for the day. We had a great time. I knew that after our visit to their home that she was someone that I wanted to get to know better. We have so much in common. But that can be discussed later. What really was the center of our conversation was Harry!"

"Tell me about it." Barclay was all ears to hear what was coming.

"Annie told me that she and Harry had spent considerable time last week talking about how he was struggling with his life…something he had never opened up about with her in the past."

"What kind of struggles, Faith?"

"Oh, how he was feeling unhappy with his radio show, how he felt that he was being dishonest with his audience, how it all seemed so artificial, so, as he put it 'phoney.' Annie said that she listened mostly, but now and then asked him to go a little deeper into what he was trying to say to her. Finally, she said that he came right out and said it. 'I'm having a crisis of faith and I don't know what to do about it.'"

"Do you know how Annie replied to this revelation of his?"

"Yes, she advised him to call you. I don't know if he took her advice, but I thought it was a good suggestion."

Barclay decided not to pursue the conversation with Faith. After all, Harry had already made the appointment to see him at St. Bartholomew's. Now he knew what Harry's visit was likely about. But there are times when even a rector does not tell anyone about certain things going on in the parish...not even his spouse. Confidentiality must be protected at all costs.

"That was interesting, wasn't it Faith? I'm glad that you and Annie had a great time shopping. Did you buy anything I'd be interested in?"

"I bought a blueberry pie. Do you want dessert tonight?"

CHAPTER SEVENTEEN

TUESDAY morning Harry arrived in Barclay's office early…fifteen minutes early, in fact. He had three coffees in tow along with a bag of apple critters, which he was already sharing with Hannah when Barclay came out of his office to meet him. Hannah and Harry were having a great time together, it appeared…both drinking coffee and eating critters, and, if Barclay was correct, talking about the local Tangleville baseball team. It seemed that Harry had discovered that Hannah was an avid fan of the Tangleville Turbos, and Barclay was reluctant to intrude. This was a side of Harry he had never witnessed before…the jovial, warm, open individual carrying on a friendly conversation with a complete stranger. After all, he and Hannah had never met before this morning. This Harry was an enigma, full of surprises, he decided. "What is next?" he wondered.

"Morning, Canon!" Harry jumped up to grasp Barclay's hand. "Here's your coffee with double cream. I hope you like a little cholesterol with your coffee!"

"Come on in Harry. Let's sit down in my office. Thanks for the treats."

"Yes, thanks from me too Mr. Sting," said Hannah.

"Let's continue our conversation sometime in the future. By the way, I really loved your last show at AM KNOW. Great stuff!"

"Thanks, Hannah…by the way, just call me Harry." Hannah smiled that warm, engaging smile of hers as she went back to work on the parish computer.

Behind the closed doors of the rector's office Barclay and Harry sat in the two big black leather chairs facing one another. A coffee table separated the chairs and Harry placed the coffee and critters down on it. They drank their coffees, snacked on a few of the calorie-loaded treats, and enjoyed a time of easy, non-controversial conversation. Barclay waited for Harry to get to the point of his requested visit.

"Doctor," Harry at last blurted out, "I'm no gambler!"

"Did I ever suggest you were?" replied Barclay.

"No, you didn't, but during the last show we did together… remember the one that dealt with atheism and faith and such, you asked the question…at least you implied that if one really was to think about whether there is a God, or not, and then to risk saying there isn't one was gambling with the consequences of eternal damnation. You really touched a cord with that. At the time I was really annoyed with you for your response. But, I couldn't get it out of my mind after the show. I went home and asked Annie how she felt about your answer. She caught a bit of the show with Faith as they were driving to the Tangleville Mall. She said that for years she wanted to say the same thing to me, but she, bless her heart, was, she told me, afraid of my response to her religious suggestions. You know that I told you that she is an Orthodox Christian. And what makes it worse is that she told me that she was praying for the time when I would become ready to open up to hearing about God in my life. Well, the time has come, Canon.

I've decided I'm no gambler. Annie's prayers have been answered. I'm here today to talk to you. I don't know where to go with my problem."

Barclay could tell that Harry was deadly serious, truly troubled in spirit. This was no time for him to respond by saying something that would seem trite or clichéd to Harry. Harry needed to be heard… this was as close to confession as Harry had probably ever come in his entire life. Barclay let Harry continue.

"Go on Harry, I'm listening."

Confessions are never to be made public by the priest. Harry was aware of this and over a period of fifty minutes he continued to pour out his past sins to Barclay. It was evident that Harry was genuine in his search for spiritual meaning in his life. He had not been baptized as a baby and of course had not become a confirmed Christian. At the close of their time together Barclay held Harry's hand and Harry read the words from the Prayer Book, the words of a penitent:

> *Most merciful God, have mercy upon me. In your com-passion forgive my sins, both known and unknown, things done and left undone, especially* (This took a full eight minutes for Harry to complete.) O *God, uphold me by your Spirit that I may live and serve you in newness of life, for the honour and glory of your name; through Jesus Christ our Lord. Amen.*

After they said The Lord's Prayer together Barclay gave Harry absolution, the assurance that his sins were forgiven by God, and they stood up, embraced, and wept together.

"The Lord has put away all your sins, Harry. Thanks be to God."

The two sat in silence in Barclay's office for a good five minutes. Harry's face was drenched in tears and he reached for additional tissues contained in a box on the coffee table separating the two big leather chairs that the two men occupied.

Barclay finally broke the silence. "Harry, you now have a few necessary steps to take. They are extremely important. Don't put them off. First and foremost, you must confide in Annie what has taken place here in this office today. Hold nothing back. I'm absolutely certain that she will be overjoyed to hear of your confession. Don't go into details as to what you said before God and me. Simply tell her of how you have confessed Jesus Christ as Lord and Saviour. Will you do that?"

"She won't be in until about four o'clock this afternoon, but I'll do exactly what you suggest the moment she gets home."

"And Harry, it is absolutely fundamental that you prepare yourself for baptism. Talk to Annie about that…where, how, and when this can be done. Then, confirmation must be pursued. In the meantime, seek out a church where you can worship on Sundays. You won't be able to take the Eucharist until you are baptized and confirmed, but you need to continue your spiritual journey…a regular worship pattern, even enrolling in a Bible Study Group, getting to know some Christian mentors, establishing a regular, routine prayer life. Annie will be able to steer you in the direction you need to go. After all, she is such a mature, devout Christian. And of course, I'm always going to be here to help you in every way I am needed. Got it, Harry?"

"Got it! Come on, Doctor, let's do lunch. My treat." Barclay readily accepted.

Chapter Eighteen

"**BARCLAY**," Faith asked, "how long has it been since Harry started attending St. Bart's? I've lost track of that day when he showed up for worship. Do you remember the surprise of the congregation when he walked into the nave and sat down in the front pew?"

"I remember it so well, Faith. It was the first Sunday in June, six months ago. Harry had not told me that he was coming that day, even though we had regularly been having coffee together each week for a good three months. I kind of suspected that he'd show up some morning. I knew that he had been attending worship with Annie at her church. But, as you know, Annie attends the Russian Orthodox parish in town, and most of the liturgy is in Russian. Harry had confided in me that he was kind of at a loss there, not being able to join in with Annie in the liturgy on Sunday mornings. He feels right at home with us at St. Bartholomew's. I only wish that he and Annie could somehow sit together on Sunday mornings. You and she are great friends, aren't you? Has she ever mentioned that this is a problem for her?"

"Yes, she has. But at the moment she says that she is only so pleased to have Harry attending worship that it doesn't matter to her where he attends church…at least for the time being."

"Harry tells me that she will be with us next Sunday when he is baptized and the Sunday following when Bishop Strictman comes for confirmation. Isn't it hard to believe how God has worked in Harry's life? Harry Sting, to be a baptized and confirmed Anglican! Who would have even thought of it when I first started sparring with him on his radio show that first time months and months ago? Harry and I have been working together weekly now for five months preparing for his baptism and confirmation. He has been reading everything I have put in his hands about the denomination, the meaning of taking his baptismal vows, confirmation, Christian discipleship, his new role as a witnessing Christian in this secular world. Every time we meet he has a question or two for me to help clarify what it means to be a practising Christian. He possesses such a great mind. Bishop Strictman has told me that he is eager to meet him. Knowing our bishop, I think that he has some plans for Harry to be used in the diocese. Harry has such great gifts to offer to the church."

St. Bartholomew's was packed for Harry's baptism. Every pew was filled and the ushers had to put chairs in the side aisles for the service. Annie, radiant in her expensive attire, sat beside him in the front pew, along with the other gathered families who were present as well for the five infant baptisms that took place. After the service Barclay, Faith, Harry, and Annie went out for brunch together downtown. Annie picked up the bill.

Bishop Strictman invited Harry to a private meeting in the bishop's office one week following his confirmation. Harry had confided in Barclay that he had no idea why the meeting had been called, but that he had readily accepted the invitation. The two talked together over their weekly coffee gathering the two days before Harry was to meet the bishop. Barclay had reassured Harry that the bishop was very impressed with him at the time of his confirmation and that the bishop had been kept abreast of their times together on The Harry Sting Show at AM KNOW.

"It must have something to do with your communication skills," Barclay suggested to Harry. "The Bishop is a pretty progressive individual. I'll bet that he will have a rather unique proposal to discuss with you. Just go and be yourself. I can't wait to talk to you when you get back."

The day after Barclay and Harry had met for coffee Hannah was surprised by the unexpected appearance of Sarah Davis who had just walked into the outer office of St. Bartholomew's unannounced. She was crying and Hannah could readily see that the makeup around her left eye was smudged, failing to cover up what was obviously a blackened eye.

"I've got to see Dr. Steadmore right now. Is he in?"

"Sarah, what happened? Are you all right? Can I get you something to drink? Are you in pain?

"I can't talk to you. I need to see the Canon. I know that he is here...his Jeep is out there in the parking lot."

Hannah knocked on Barclay's door. She knew that he was preparing for his coming weekly homily at this point in the week doing research for the first draft. After every sermon that was preached on Sunday, a published manuscript of the homily would be typed up by Hannah and made available for worshippers to take home the following Sunday to be distributed to friends and shut-ins who did not attend or could not be present for Sunday worship. A mailing list was kept at St. Bartholomew's of people who received the homily by mail, some as far away as Brookfield Commons. She hated to interrupt Barclay, but she knew that this was a crisis situation for Sarah. "Doctor, Sarah Davis is here. I think you had better see her!"

"Show her in, Hannah. Can you find out if she drinks tea or coffee and bring in a cup for each of us? And, as usual, don't leave the office while Sarah and I meet here in my office. Walk by the open window now and then to let Sarah know that you are out there. Hannah nodded: she knew the routine to let a visitor in Barclay's office know that the rector was not alone in the church, especially if the rector and the individual for counseling were of the opposite sex. Times had changed from former years when clergy were seldom accused of improper conduct. The Bishop had issued strict procedures for his clergy to follow when in counseling those in crisis situations. Barclay was simply following his Bishop's instructions.

Hannah gently knocked on Barclay's door, with Sarah following closely behind. Barclay got up, opened the door, and greeted Sarah.

"Sarah, take this comfortable chair here by the coffee table. I'll take the other big one. Let's talk!" Sarah's chair was placed in such a position that when occupied the person seated in it faced the large window separating the rector's door from the outer office where Hannah held down the reception areas of the administration section of the church. By this time Sarah's makeup was thoroughly smudged. Tears were streaming down her face as she held a handful of facial tissues in her left hand, trying to cover her left blackened eye. Barclay waited for her to compose herself, which seemed to take longer than he had expected. At last, she broke the silence.

"Bill came in late this morning, drunk as usual, and immediately demanded my attention for sex. I refused his advances, and he pulled me over on my back and struck me three times with his fist, the last strike right over my eye. I screamed, and I don't know how I found the strength, but managed to push him away, run to the bathroom downstairs next to the den, locked the door and shook uncontrollably for twenty minutes. I fully expected him to follow me. I thought that he might try to break down the door, but he didn't. I finally came out of the bathroom and curled up on the sofa in the den. When I awoke this morning, I tried to cover up this eye with makeup, but I couldn't stop crying. I knew that I had to talk with you. I'm sorry that I'm such a mess. I don't know what to do."

"I suspect, Sarah, that this has been going on for some time now. Do you remember the time that you spoke to me from the drive-through window some months ago when I ordered coffee? Remember how I asked you to postpone your upcoming marriage because of Bill's abuse? Even though you two have since moved in together, it's only gotten worse, hasn't it? Now is the time for you to make some difficult decisions. Are you ready to make some difficult decisions?"

"Am I ready?" Sarah blurted out. "Where do I start?"

"First of all, do you need medical attention? Do you want me to arrange to get you to a medical clinic for the professional assessment of your injuries? That will be absolutely invaluable if you proceed to press charges against Bill. You have every right to do so. In fact, you must!"

"No, no! I'm all right. This black eye will heal. I don't want to get Bill in trouble. I think that he can change, if I just give him more time. The wedding plans are almost in place. Please, Doctor, just talk to Bill. Please!"

"Sarah, talking to Bill is not going to work at this point. It is you that has to take action. You can't cover up for him any longer. He will only respond according to how you take control. First and foremost, you must move out of the house…immediately. Have you anywhere you can go?"

"No, Canon, I've no place to go. My parents live six hundred miles away and I want to keep my job at the coffee shop. I can't afford not to work. Bill and I need the money."

"Sarah, Bill's problems right now are not your concern. It is you that matters. Bill is only going to respond when he finds out you are not enabling his present lifestyle. You must postpone the wedding. You must separate now. I can get you into a women's shelter right this day. Let me do it. Let me make the call."

"But Bill will not like it. He may come after me. What then?"

"Sarah, listen to me. Stop protecting Bill. You will be safe…absolutely safe at the Safe Haven's Women Shelter. One of my parishioners is the CEO in charge. She will make sure that you are safe there. The police and the shelter have a direct call service line in effect. You have to take the first step. Let me call Safe Haven's."

"What about my clothes? My personal belongings at home? Bill won't like it a bit."

"They have everything you will need for a few days. Let's wait to see how Bill responds to your moving out. That is going to tell us a lot about how much he loves you, misses you. If he doesn't respond, then you will know for certain that your upcoming wedding has to be cancelled. We'll put Bill to the test."

There was a gentle knock on Barclay's office door, and Hannah entered with a tray holding two coffee cups, cream and sugar, and a plate of blueberry muffins that she had brought into the office that morning.

"Ah, Hannah! Thank you. Sarah, let's have a coffee. Hannah's muffins are to die for."

Sarah smiled ever so slightly. "I'll bet they are better than the ones we sell at the coffee shop where I work!" She needed no encouragement to take the first bite, and to sip from her mug of coffee.

This gave Barclay a few minutes while they ate together to make the next suggestion to Sarah. After Hannah exited the office, Barclay continued. "Sarah, will you go to Safe Haven's?"

"I guess that I have no choice, have I?." she replied. "But where do we go from here?"

"We'll meet in a couple of days at the shelter. They have a wonderful little chapel there. By that time we will see how Bill responds to your moving out. What do you say?"

"Make the call, Canon. I feel good making the first move. Will you pray with me for God to lead me into the future?"

Barclay invited Sarah to close her eyes and fold her hands together and he prayed a prayer of thanksgiving that Sarah was able to take the initiative to make the first step to a new beginning from her abusive relationship with Bill. Barclay prayed for guidance for both Sarah and Bill, and they closed together by repeating the Lord's Prayer. Barclay gave Sarah a blessing and they both ended the prayer with a joint pronunciation of "amen."

Sarah was smiling for the second time that morning. Barclay arranged for Hannah to drive Sarah to Safe Haven's after he called to arrange for her residency.

"I wonder what Bill will do now that Sarah has moved out," Barclay thought to himself. This could be quite a life-altering turn of events for both of them.

The phone rang. Hannah was out of the office on the way to Safe Haven's. The call display on his phone told him that it was Harry Sting's cell phone number calling.

"Hello, Harry. What's up?"

CHAPTER NINETEEN

"**CANON,** we've got to meet. I met with Bishop Strictman yesterday and I need to talk something over with you. Can we get together over lunch?"

"Can't make it for lunch, Harry. I've got hospital visits to do today and some administrative duties that just have been piling up on my desk. Can it wait until about three thirty this afternoon? We can meet here in my office."

"Okay, that will have to do. Double cream, right? Will Hannah still be there in the office? I'll bring a coffee for her as well."

"No, she finishes at two o'clock today. You will have to ring the bell to tell me that you have arrived. I'll hear it in my office and let you in. Hannah locks up after she leaves."

"I'll be there, Doctor. I can't wait to get your opinion on something."

It was wonderful to see Harry so enthusiastic about his life. What a change from the old cynical, confrontational Harry Sting that was portrayed during his pre-Christian days at AM KNOW.

Barclay finished sorting out the morning mail, answered sixteen emails, and completed the rough draft of the weekly bulletin for Hannah to work on over the next three days. "Hannah, I'm off to the hospitals.

I'll keep my phone on and you can get me if something urgent comes up. Don't book anything from three thirty on. Harry is coming in and I think that I'll need some considerable time to spend with him."

"Will do. Give my regards to Harry. I really like that fellow."

There it was again. The new Harry Sting…the charmer, the fellow whose real inner warmth, hidden for so long, was now attracting new friends and admiration wherever he went. Who says that a wolf can't be trusted with the lambs? As Isaiah the prophet put it:

> *The wolf shall live with the lamb, the leopard shall lie down with the kid…. (Isaiah 11:6)*

Barclay spent the next three hours at Tangleville's hospital visiting St. Bartholomew's parishioners admitted for observation and, in some cases, upcoming surgery. What a privilege it is for a priest to attend the bedside of the parish sick and suffering, anointing the sick for healing, bringing Holy Communion to the faithful, holding the hand of the patient lying there, often with the gathered concerned family members who are present as well, all joining hands together in a circle of prayer with their loved one. The priest prays for healing, for control of pain, for faith for all that the risen Lord is present and that the medical staff will properly diagnose and prescribe the correct treatment for recovery. It is always so obvious that together prayer, sacrament, and modern medicine work miracles. Canon Steadmore had witnessed many occasions when the words in the Letter of James reaped a miraculous return to health.

> *Are any among you sick? They should call for the elders of the church, and have them pray over them, anointing them with oil in the name of the Lord. The prayer of faith will save the sick , and the Lord will raise them*

up; and anyone who has committed sins will be forgiven.
(James 5:14-15)

The morning passed quickly. Hospital visits always take longer than expected because in towns where well-known rectors are recognizable by a great number of people, a visiting cleric always encounters people in the sick wards who are not perhaps members of one's parish, but who nevertheless wish to spend a few minutes together, often even asking for prayer as well. That is precisely what took place that morning as Doctor Steadmore made his rounds. He managed to grab a quick lunch in one of the hospital's cafeterias and then drove back to St. Bart's Parish. Hannah left the office at two and the caretaker, Chuck Edelson, had already finished his daily duties. Hannah had left a note on Barclay's desk: "Don't forget that Harry S. is coming at three thirty. See you tomorrow, Hannah. P.S. Give him my greetings!" Barclay smiled. It was obvious that Harry had made a strong impression with Hannah. That was the new Harry, all right.

Barclay had just settled into the most unenjoyable task of a rector, parish administration, when the doorbell rang. Barclay glanced at his watch, and it read two thirty-seven. "Harry must be early," Barclay thought to himself. "I'll never get this office paperwork caught up." he mumbled as he walked to the front of the office to unlock the door.

There stood Bill Bilker, Sarah Davis' live-in boyfriend. It was obvious by his unkempt attire and his unsteady stance that he had been drinking heavily.

"I need to see you, Doctor Steadmore. Can I come in?" His slurred speech was slow and disordered.

"Bill, how did you get here?" asked a surprised Barclay. "Did Sarah drop you off?"

"No, I have a car. It is out there in the parking lot. Sarah is at work, I think. Can I talk to you?"

"What do you mean, she is at work, you think? Don't you know where she is?"

"She left me last night. I don't know where she is staying. Can I come in?"

There was no way that Barclay was going to let Bill drive anywhere in the condition he appeared to be in. "Come in, Bill. I've got a pot of coffee brewing. Let me get you a cup."

Barclay steered Bill into one of the big leather chairs in his office and told him to sit there until he returned with the coffee. It was obvious that anything he was about to say to Bill was going to go right over his head, judging from the inebriated state he was in. The best thing he could do for the next hour or so was to try to sober Bill up, listen to his story, and arrange for a ride for him back to his house. There was no way Bill was fit to get back into his car and drive.

For the next fifty minutes Bill poured out his story to Barclay, all the while consuming three cups of strong coffee. Barclay listened, only interjecting now and then to have Bill clarify what had transpired between him and Sarah. Bill did not at first admit to striking Sarah, until well past the first half-hour of conversation. Finally, with tears streaming down his face, he admitted to his violent past with her. He confessed that he had been up all night and spent all morning at a downtown bar.

"Help me, Doctor. I love her. I don't think she'll come back. What am I going to do?"

"Bill, I want you to go home. Get some sleep. Call me tomorrow and we'll continue to talk. Don't come here drinking. Do you hear me? Right now we're going to have a prayer together."

Bill struggled to his feet as Barclay prayed, ending with the two of them repeating the Lord's Prayer. Bill excused himself to go to the bathroom and Barclay reached to the phone to call the peoples' warden, Sergeant Gideon Hopewell, the long-time member of the Tangleville Police Force. If Gideon was off duty, Barclay knew that he could count on him to drive Bill home and not to report him to the local precinct. In the past Gideon had stepped in to bail out parishioners at St. Bartholomew's many times. Gideon, a devout Christian, was a man of compassion and grace. The answering service cut in and Gideon's voice indicated that he was not available at the time. "Please leave a message and call back later." Before Barclay could leave a brief message, Bill returned to the office, just as the main office doorbell rang.

"Sit down Bill, I'll get it!"

Barclay closed his office door behind him, and proceeded to the front entrance to the foyer of St. Bartholomew's office complex. It was Harry Sting, right on time, holding two cups of coffee and a bag that Barclay knew contained two apple critters.

"Harry, before we go into the office, we've got to talk, right now. Keep your voice down. Just listen. I've got Bill Bilken in my office. He is in no condition to drive. I want you to drive him home right now. Share those coffees together and don't argue with him. He is still quite drunk. He may object, but I'll give him no choice but to go with you. When he went to the bathroom he left his car keys in the chair. I've got them and he is not going to get them back until he sobers up. Are you up to it?"

"Barclay, I've never told you, but I'm a sober, twenty-year member of AA. Leave it to me. God works in mysterious ways, doesn't He? By the way, you didn't know that I wore that hat, did you?"

"You are a man of many surprises, Harry. We'll need to re-schedule our meeting for today. How about tomorrow for lunch?"

"You're on and it's on me."

CHAPTER TWENTY

BARCLAY arrived at the office early the next morning, a Friday. He spent the entire forenoon attempting to catch up on the office administrative load that he had not been able to complete the day before. He expected Bill Bilker to arrive to reclaim his car keys, but Bill didn't call or show up. "That's strange," thought Barclay. "I wonder what that means."

It was a productive morning and not a single person unexpectedly arrived to cut into Barclay's time. By eleven forty-five he called Hannah into the office and together they went over the coming week's agenda. He had asked Hannah to hold all calls that were not urgent and asked if she had arranged for him to reply to those which needed to be returned.

"It was a quiet morning," replied Hannah. "Nothing I couldn't handle. Only a couple of calls enquiring about the times for Sunday services. However, a car pulled into the parking lot around ten this morning, dropped off someone and left. I didn't catch who it was. Then a second car left. Do you know anything about that?"

"Bill Bilker! That's got to be who it was! I bet that he had a second set of keys at home and reclaimed his car. It is a long story Hannah. We haven't heard the last of it yet."

Harry Sting walked into the outer office foyer and poked his head through Barclay's open office door. "Good morning, Hannah. To you too, Canon. I'll wait out here until you two are finished."

"Oh, we're finished, Mr. Sting. I'll join you." She hurriedly rose from her chair and proceeded to her office desk and Harry sat down in one of the outer office chairs.

It was obvious that the two of them needed a few minutes together. In their animated conversation, Barclay could overhear that they were discussing last night's Tangleville Turbos' baseball game. Barclay deliberately stalled for time to let the two of them engage in conversation. It was wonderful to see the two of them in the office enjoying their time together, laughing and arguing over who was at fault in the Turbos' loss. Finally Barclay interrupted the two of them and reminded Harry that they had a luncheon date together. Harry seemed reluctant to end his conversation with Hannah, but slowly stood to his feet, smiling. They said their goodbyes and he reminded her that the conversation was not over. Hannah readily agreed.

On the way to Barclay's favorite restaurant, The Red Pagoda, Tangleville's choice place for Chinese food, Barclay, the passenger in Harry's white BMW, was all ears to learn how Harry had gotten along yesterday when he took Bill Bilker home from the office.

"I took the longer way to his house," Harry replied, "just to give him a little more time to sober up, and to give me an opportunity to listen to his story. He was desperately afraid that Sarah's and his relationship was over. She had not contacted him since she moved out and he was quite concerned that he might be reported to the police for giving her that beating last week. We finally got around to the drinking, but he denied even having a problem. I told him about my twenty years of sobriety and that I would be happy to sponsor him through AA, but he was having nothing of it. He's in bad shape."

"Don't I know it. One of these days he is going to get arrested for impaired driving and end up in jail. Let's hope that he doesn't kill or maim some innocent person or seriously injure himself."

They continued their conversation en route to the Red Pagoda. It was obvious to Barclay that Harry was very concerned over Bill's problems.

Barclay could never have imagined that back when he started out as a guest on his show at AM KNOW Harry Sting would become this new person in Christ...passionate about the needs of a total stranger, giving of his time to assist others, jovial, warm, and kind. What a lesson to learn. Christ changes people, so to prejudge someone is so unchristian. Conversion is a powerful factor for the transformation of the human psyche.

The maître d' at the Red Pagoda ushered Harry and Barclay to a secluded table at the far end of the restaurant...a great place for private conversation. Harry ordered Chinese tea for two and after they both returned from the buffet area Barclay said the blessing over the meal. Harry concluded the grace with an audible 'amen' and crossed himself. Barclay inwardly smiled.

"All right, Harry, what is up with your visit with Bishop Strictman?"

Harry was beaming from ear to ear. "Are you ready for this, Doctor? The bishop had a proposal to offer to me."

"Okay, Harry, I'm all ears."

"He wants me to oversee a new program in the diocese with the title of Communications Director. I will need a half-dozen people, handpicked people, to work with me. They may be ordained, or laity, or a combination of both. The objective is to make the Diocese of

New Avondale better known to the general public, what our denomination stands for, and our mission to the world. But what is really exciting is that the bishop wants me to oversee the establishment of a rehabilitation complex right here in Tangleville…a place for recovery from addiction to alcohol and drugs. Of course, money will have to be raised for the construction of such a complex. The diocese has the funds for a media blitz, but not for mortar and bricks. With my exposure in broadcasting he thinks that I am the man for the task. I'm overwhelmed that he has offered me this position. I don't know what to say to him. I asked for a week to think about it before I give him my answer."

"Harry, I'm not surprised to hear this. Bishop Strictman is a very astute man, one who is an excellent judge of character and of one's potential to excel in whatever role God calls one to take on for the church. I wouldn't be surprised that somehow he was aware of your long association with AA. Your confession to me was a complete surprise, but bishops seem to have ways of knowing about people and the events going on in their dioceses. You are eminently qualified for the task with your knowledge of the media and your exposure to addictions. But what about Annie? Does she support such a new undertaking?"

"I'll say that she does! She, as you know, is financially well off, and she told me yesterday that she has been trying to decide now for some time on a worthy cause to support. She is excited over the possible establishment of an addiction center here in Tangleville. She right up front told me that she will donate an initial one hundred thousand dollars to the project. I'm so excited that she is on side."

"Have you told the Bishop about Annie's willingness to kick-start the project?"

"No, I haven't. We're still talking about whether I will take the job."

"Have you prayed over such an appointment?"

"Yes! Last evening during our family devotions, we committed the entire concept to God. We're just about ready to decide together what to do."

"Look, Harry, I'm sure that God will reveal to both of you the way to go. As for me, I think that you are the man for the task. Of course, Annie has to be there by your side. And I don't only mean as a financial contributor. I mean as a team member of the undertaking... somewhere in the organization."

"Thanks, Doctor. I needed to hear that. Let's go back for a second time to the buffet area. I want us to get our money's worth today."

"Harry, I'll bet that Annie would never say such a thing. But right now, I'm with you."

Harry grinned as he led Barclay back to the food area. The kitchen had just replaced the empty crab legs tray.

Chapter Twenty-One

FAITH and Barclay finished their Friday evening dinner and had retreated to comfortable chairs in their family den. A blazing log fire was burning in the fireplace and both of them were still drinking their second cup of dark roast coffee...double cream for Barclay and single cream for Faith. They hadn't spoken for over a five-minute period as they enjoyed their time together. Both knew how blessed they were...a great marriage, no real financial difficulties, a paid off mortgage, and the realization that their ministry at St. Bartholomew's over the past ten years had blossomed beyond their wildest expectations. Barclay and Faith had even, once or twice during the past two years, discussed what was next in their lives. Another appointment by Bishop Strictman? Staying at St. Bartholomew's until Barclay's retirement? After all, there were still eight years to go before Barclay was eligible to retire with a full pension.

Barclay finally broke the silence. "Faith, do you realize it has been a full year since Harry and I had that lunch date at the Red Pagoda and he informed me of Bishop Strictman's offer to appoint him as Communications Director for the diocese? And then he surprised me with the news that the bishop also wanted a rehabilitation center complex for the treatment of addictions in Tangleville."

"He certainly got right to work, didn't he?" replied Faith. "With Annie first donating that one hundred thousand dollars to kick-start the project, and with her lobbying of the Orthodox Church and some friends of financial means, that addition of two hundred and forty thousand dollars she raised certainly convinced Harry to take over the project."

"And Faith, that former motel up for sale at the edge of the town, with its three convention rooms and eighty furnished suites, just seemed to fall into the hands of the diocese, didn't it? What a perfect place for the addiction center it has become. Did you ever hear how it got its now familiar new name?"

"Annie told me that it was she who named it 'The Samaritan Inn,'" Faith answered.

"Annie knows her Bible, doesn't she? You and she have become great friends, haven't you Faith? She still worships in her Russian Orthodox parish, doesn't she? But isn't it wonderful how she attends the ten thirty service with Harry here at St. Bartholomew's? And I thought it was a stroke of genius that Harry appointed her to the board of directors at The Samaritan Inn. Harry is a smart fellow."

"Not as smart as Annie," Faith winked at Barclay. "Don't forget that behind every successful married man is his coach...his spouse." Barclay knew better than to disagree...he was not going there!

The two of them continued to reminisce about the last twelve months in Tangleville. Finally, Faith said, "I'm going up to bed to watch the final innings of the Tangleville Turbos on cable television. Will you be coming soon?"

"In a few minutes, Faith. I'm just going to watch the fire die down and I'll be up."

Faith gave Barclay a pat on the neck as she left for the bedroom. Barclay pushed his big leather chair into a reclining position, his feet elevated before him, and continued to gaze at the dying embers of the fire. His mind drifted back to the previous activities of last year.

So many things had taken place…many of them totally unexpected. Bill Bilker, in a drunken state, wrecked his new pickup truck, striking another car and injuring its senior driver. The victim survived, but spent four months in rehabilitation learning to walk again. Bill went to court, and of course, lost his driver's license for a year's duration. In two months from now he may get it back, but his insurance rates will be astronomically high. The fact that he finally agreed to go to AA with Harry was a godsend. Bill confided in Barclay that he has been an abstainer now for a four-month period. In a strange twist of fate, Harry had offered Bill a permanent position at The Samaritan Inn as a front desk staff member, the first person new admissions to the addiction center had to deal with on entrance to any particular program at the center. Bill was doing a superb job, taking his new position seriously, with a great deal of pride in doing so.

Sarah had finally come to the conclusion that staying with her abusive live-in boyfriend was not a wise choice. Eight months ago she enrolled in a course at the Tangleville Community College and will graduate as a personal support worker. She attends St. Bartholomew's on a regular basis, always at the eight o'clock morning service to avoid meeting Bill who now attends the ten o'clock liturgy. She still works part-time evenings and weekends at the local drive-thru coffee shop. With the help of a student loan, and with careful management of her finances, she is going to make it. She will have a profession, a steady income and a new sense of self-worth. Good for Sarah!

Harry was granted permission to revamp his radio show at AM KNOW. Barclay remembered how Harry had struggled with what to do with his popular show after his new-found faith in Christianity and how Harry had decided that if the station management would permit it, he would drastically re-format the segments of his daily airtime. Barclay was not sure how this would come about, if indeed it was to happen.

Leave it to Harry. He convinced the station that instead of being the old rabble-rouser talk show host, that he would instead mold the show into an educational two-hour event. The first hour Harry interviewed highly respected authorities in various fields on the topic of the day, and in the second hour the air waves were opened to the listening audience to ask the guest questions that they wanted answered.

Topics that increased his ratings included assisted suicide, secularism, abortion, euthanasia, embryonic stem cell research, and human cloning. But the shows that really advanced his popularity in the listening audience involved local medical doctors discussing issues that potentially affected the listening audience...controversies about vaccines, C-sections, mammograms, circumcision, and electroshock treatment.

Harry had evolved into a skilled interviewer. It was obvious that he researched each topic prior to the show of the day and asked questions of each guest that conveyed that he was aware of what the listening audience might be wanting to ask the visitor. Gone were the days when Harry tried to put his visitors on the spot. No longer was he trying to one-up them, and the listening audience was beginning to take him seriously. He was being asked with ever-increasing regularity to be the guest speaker at social events in Tangelville...even invited to do so at church functions, where before he would never have been allowed to cross the threshold of such communities. Ecumenicalism now trumped secularism.

The odometer on Harry's BMW was climbing. Bishop Strictman, in inviting Harry to be the Communications Director for the diocese, was using him at every opportunity, whenever there was the need for professional handling of public relations with the media. Harry revelled in doing so, diffusing possible controversial issues that the secular press, through television and radio scrums, often seemed too intent on being "got you" opportunities. The old Harry was still there, just below the surface. "I wonder if it still felt exhilarating?" mused Barclay as he smiled to himself.

"Barclay, the Turbos just won and are now going to advance to the finals!" Faith's voice was jubilant as she yelled downstairs.

The last glowing embers were almost out in the fireplace, and after saying his evening prayers Barclay retired to their upstairs bedroom. A final kiss with Faith and he turned out the bedside lamp.

Just as he was about to nod off his cell phone rang. It was the Tangleville hospital chaplain on the line. "Canon, Joe Fields is dying and the family has gathered at his bedside. They are requesting that you come in and anoint Mr. Fields for dying. I know that it's late, but they say that they are family members of St. Bartholomew's. What should I tell them?"

"I'll be there in thirty minutes."

EPILOGUE

THE question arises, and it is now answered: Where is Tangleville? Tangleville is just about any place, anywhere. Wherever Christians reside, the challenge of living out the teachings of Christ in the secular world emerges in ways that entangle the hopes, dreams, special interests, and conflicting agendas of the diverse, at-odds citizenry, for all wear different "hats," so to speak...hats that identify a community's members as to whom and how each one may wish to be known, hats that may proclaim whether one promotes a certain political party, a specific religious affiliation, a mover or a shaker in the crowd, a secular humanist, or a person who perhaps marches to his or her own drumbeat.

The citizenry of every Tangleville, wherever such communities may be located, always have choices to make, just as Harry Sting, Canon Doctor Steadmore, Annie Antonov-Sting, Bill Bilker, Bishop Strictman...indeed, each of the residents of their home town, had to wrestle with who they were, their problems, their biases, their personal ambitions and agendas. The passing of time itself opens and closes doors that lead to paths and opportunities that one initially may have thought to be impossible, or, at the very least, unlikely.

Doctor Steadmore and Faith retired from ministry at St. Bartholomew's, sold their home and bought a high-rise condo in Trinity Harbour, one hundred and ten miles from Tangleville. They both attend the local parish near their new residence, and occasionally Doctor Steadmore takes services for the rector when he is needed. Faith volunteers twice a week in the tuck shop of the local hospital. Both enjoy good health and have traded in the old Jeep Liberty for a new Mustang convertible. Two old fogies, they admit, who are still young at heart.

Harry Sting has witnessed unexpected but needed growth at The Samaritan Inn, now expanded to two hundred beds, accommodating both adult and juvenile admissions.

Bishop Strictman, with one more year remaining as Bishop of New Avondale, made Harry a lay Canon in the Diocese. Annie continues to raise funds for the treatment center, while serving as the chair of the financial committee of the non-profit organization, still officially affiliated with the Diocese of New Avondale.

Sting's radio show continues to be the most listened to broadcast in Tangleville and the surrounding areas, informative and educational through the high quality of guests as Harry continues to invite the movers and shakers of the community to his show. No longer is his audience divided into opposing groups who previously listened only to be amused by the controversy he was able to stir up during his broadcasts. The 'sting' aspect of his show is no longer there, and Harry considered a more appropriate stage surname for the show. Annie is strongly opposed to such a move as she claims that it would be a denial of her husband's transformation…the work of God in his life. Harry is now in great demand as a theme speaker at many of Tangleville's social functions and always skillfully interjects some aspect of his Christian faith into his presentations.

The new rector at St. Bartholomew's, the Reverend Canon Matthew Hudson, is a dynamic priest, a family man with Margaret, better known to close friends as Maggie, his vivacious, prosecuting attorney spouse, and four children…three girls and a boy. The parish is thriving under his leadership with a growing Sunday school, an active youth group, and weekly classes for new adherents preparing for baptism, confirmation, or transference of membership from other Christian denominations. Canon Hudson honored Doctor Steadmore by inviting him to be an honorary associate priest at St. Bartholomew's, and Dr. Steadmore was delighted to accept the invitation. Even though Faith and he live some distance away, they attend St. Bartholomew's on church high days, and Doctor Steadmore vests for the morning liturgies.

Each year Harry and Barclay have maintained a long-established tradition of sending through the mail a hat…usually a baseball cap… on each other's birthdays, just to reminisce about the good old days on Harry's radio show when Barclay used to ask Harry, "Which hat do you want me to wear in answering that question?"

The hat Barclay most recently received bore a quote from John Oldham across the front:

"All your future lies beneath your hat."

When Faith saw Barclay wearing it for the first time, she said, "There must be a sermon somewhere in that statement, don't you think?"

Smiling at her, Barclay nodded in agreement!

About the Author

 **DONALD** H. Hull was born on an eastern Ontario dairy farm. In his early years he taught at the elementary school level and later as a high school math teacher in Ottawa, Ontario. In mid-life he pursued a change of career, leading to ordination as an Anglican priest in the Diocese of Huron, and went on to serve as rector of an active downtown church in Windsor. After completing his Doctor of Ministry degree, the Reverend Canon Dr. Hull became principal at Canterbury College, an Anglican institution affiliated with the University of Windsor. There he taught New Testament Studies to those pursuing degrees in Theology and Religious Studies until his retirement in 2008. Dr. Hull continues to lecture on a part-time basis. A serious woodworker as well as photography and sports car enthusiast, Dr. Hull lives with his wife Faye, with whom he has recently celebrated 50 years of marriage.

Printed in Canada